Cousin Lizzie's Legacy

Alice Evans

Published by

MELROSE
BOOKS

An Imprint of Melrose Press Limited
St Thomas Place, Ely
Cambridgeshire
CB7 4GG, UK
www.melrosebooks.com

FIRST EDITION

Cover designed by Gwyn Law

ISBN 978 1 907040 47 4

Printed and bound in Great Britain by:
CPI Antony Rowe. Chippenham, Wiltshire

FSC
www.fsc.org
MIX
Paper from responsible sources
FSC® C013604

Dedicated to my children for their love and encouragement.

Acknowledgements

My friend Anna Holland for researching 'Rationing and Utility Clothing of the Nineteen-Forties' and 'Nineteen-Forties Rationing – Utility Clothing Fashion and Costume History'.

My friends Barbara and Les Pratt for lending me their book on Umbria by Philip's Travel Guides.

My friend Joy Stone for reading my rough drafts and encouraging me to keep writing.

My thanks to John Farley, creative writing tutor at 'Fairkytes' and the members of the writing group for their helpful comments and constructive criticism.

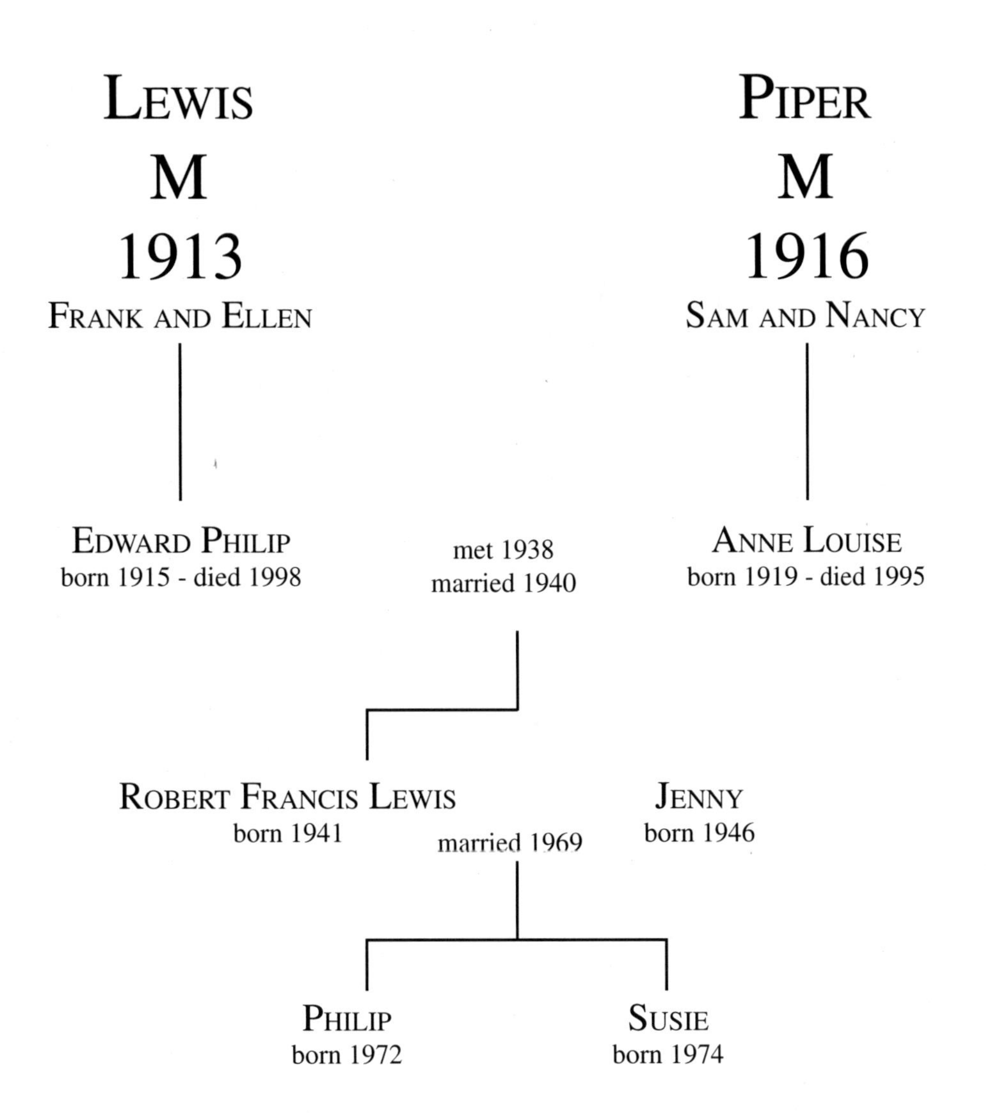

ELIZABETH LEWIS
(LIZZIE)
born 1923 - died 1998

JOAN ELIZABETH
born 1945

PAOLO CARDI
born 1922
was repatriated in 1944 after Italy surrendered

Time Scale of the Story

Prologue: 1999

Part One: 1937 – 1945

Part Two: 1999

Epilogue: 1998

PROLOGUE
1999

Joan tipped the two young removal men and saw them to the door of her newly acquired flat. She went into the sitting room and ran a hand over the bureau they had delivered. It had belonged to her mother, Anne Lewis, and before that to her grandmother, Nancy Piper, and now held pride of place in the alcove which separated the sitting room from the dining area. The bureau was rather dusty, having been in storage for some while, so Joan went to fetch a duster and beeswax polish from the hall cupboard and returned to the sitting room. She took out the bureau drawer and tipped some loose pieces of paper into a bin and dusted the inside. She tried to return the drawer to its place, but something was stuck in a groove at the back. Joan reached in and retrieved an envelope. It was rather dirty and yellowed. She took it to the dining room and sat down at the table to open it. Inside was a photo of a girl, arm in arm with a young man in an unfamiliar uniform. There was a certificate of some kind. A marriage certificate? No. A birth certificate. Joan read the name of the mother. The father was not named, but the child was: Joan Elizabeth Lewis.

So that was why Cousin Lizzie had left her the legacy.

Usually Joan found the gentle shushing of the waves ebbing and flowing on the beach beneath her bedroom window comforting. But not tonight. Her mind was in turmoil. Why had no one told her? Was the girl Lizzie? Who was the young man? The uniform he wore was not strictly military looking. Was he foreign? What had happened to him? What kind of arrangement had her mother and father come to with Cousin Lizzie? Was she adopted?

The questions came into her mind and went out one after the other like the waves breaking and receding on the beach. 'This won't do,' the sensible side of Joan told her. 'I'll deal with it in the morning. I'll phone Robert. He'll know what to do.' And with that she made a determined effort to go to sleep.

But when morning came, Joan didn't phone her brother. Perhaps he didn't know either. Instead she phoned Robert's daughter.

Susie had a sharp inquiring mind, but she also had a romantic streak in her nature and Joan thought that would come to the fore when she showed her the photograph and the birth certificate.

Susie was delighted to accept her aunt's invitation to lunch the following Sunday. She was very fond of Aunt Joan and remembered the times when she and her elder brother, Philip, had been collected from boarding school to spend holidays with Granny and Grandfather Lewis, or had been driven to various airports to join their parents, wherever their father's career in the Foreign Office had posted him. Besides she wanted to see what improvements her aunt had made to the flat which, according to the estate agent's 'blurb', was in need of some renovation.

"Come in. Come in. It's lovely to see you. Oh, you shouldn't have," said Joan as she took the bunch of daffodils Susie proffered.

"Mm, something smells nice," said Susie.

She wandered around the flat.

"I'm glad you kept Gran's bureau, Aunt Joan. It looks just right there."

"Yes," said Joan "and it held a few surprises."

"Really!" Susie raised her eyebrows.

"Yes, really," said her aunt. "Let's have lunch first, then I'll tell you all about it."

After lunch, Joan and Susie settled themselves on the sofa to drink their coffee. When they had finished, Susie said, "Well, what surprises did the bureau hold?" Joan handed Susie the envelope.

"Crumbs," Susie said when she had looked at the photograph and read the birth certificate. "What did Dad say?"

"I haven't told him yet."

"Well, I think you ought to. He kept a whole lot of Gran and Grandfather's stuff after the house was sold, you know. Papers and old photo albums. That kind of thing."

Then she looked at Joan. "What about you, Aunty? How do you feel about this? It must have come as quite a shock."

"Yes, you could say that," said Joan. "I don't quite know how I feel, or what to do. Look at that photo again. Now look at me. Am I who I think I am?"

"I think we should go and see Mum and Dad. Philip's home on leave at the moment. He'll be pleased to see you and I'm free next weekend. Yes, that's what we'll do. Can I use your phone?"

Part One

Chapter 1

Edward Lewis sat in the outer office of the editorial suite of 'The Chronicle'. The editor's secretary answered the internal phone and nodded.

"Mr. Lewis," she said. "The editor will see you now."

Edward rose confidently and went across to the inner office door and knocked.

"Come," a voice within called.

Edward opened the door and went in.

"Morning Dad."

"Morning Edward," his father answered. "Sit down." He came straight to the point of the interview. "Are you sure that this is what you want to do? Make journalism your career?"

"Yes Dad."

Edward had a vision of himself writing exciting reports for the newspaper his father edited. Living the high life. Meeting interesting people. Interviewing eminent politicians. Swapping 'scoops' with other journalists in the pub after work. But his father had other ideas.

"I'll make a few enquiries," he said. "Are you in for dinner tonight?"

"Yes Dad".

"Righto. I'll see you later then and we'll talk some more. Off you go. I need to get down to the newsroom."

Edward left the room with a smile on his face. He was twenty-two years old. Footloose and fancy-free. A good degree in Modern Languages behind him. Good job prospects in front of him.

He said "goodbye" to Miss Prior and walked out into Fleet Street.

Frank Lewis pressed the button on his intercom.

"Get me an outside line please, Miss Prior," he said.

Chapter 2

Once again Edward found himself sitting in the outer office waiting to be interviewed by the editor. Not quite the plush surroundings he had once envisaged, but a rather grotty room in a small town newspaper building, where his father had decided he would begin to learn his trade as a journalist.

Looking about him, his eyes were drawn to a calendar pinned to a noticeboard – 'Views of Elmersdale 1937' – and printed underneath the date pad was the name of a funeral director.

John Perry opened the door of his office and viewed a somewhat dejected looking Edward Lewis. He hid a grin behind his handkerchief, pretending to blow his nose.

"Cunning old devil, Frank Lewis," he thought. "Knew his stuff though, otherwise he wouldn't be the editor of 'The Chronicle' while here I am, editor and proprietor of the 'Elmersdale Gazette'."

"Edward," he called. "Come into the office. George, get us two teas, sharpish."

George, a spotty faced, bespectacled youth sitting at a desk littered with old files, various old copies of local and London newspapers and other unspeakable detritus, got to his feet and ambled off into a small kitchen.

"Your father and I go back a long way," John Perry said to Edward, as they sat drinking tea strong enough for a spoon to stand up in. "We started our careers as cub reporters on the 'Somerford Post' must be all of thirty years ago. Anyway, Frank says you are bent on becoming a journalist."

"Yes sir," said Edward.

"Well, best to make a start then."

John rummaged around in a drawer in his desk and brought out a lined notebook and a couple of sharpened pencils.

"There's a funeral at the church at half past two. That will give you time to go and fix up your lodgings with Mrs. Day."

He handed Edward a piece of paper with an address on it. "There's a bike out in the yard. You can use it until you can get one of your own. Report back here at one o'clock and I'll give you a few pointers."

"How am I supposed to get home for me dinner?" said George.

"You've got legs haven't you?" said John Perry and went back into his office and closed the door.

Edward went round to the outside of the building and found an alleyway that led into the yard. The bicycle had seen better days, but it would do until he could afford to buy one for himself. He pedalled off to find Mrs. Day.

Edward rode down the main thoroughfare of Elmersdale, trying to get his bearings; making a mental note of likely looking hostelries, before stopping to enquire as to the whereabouts of the street where Mrs. Day lived. Having obtained directions, he found it and knocked on the door of a large Edwardian villa.

He was relieved to see that Mrs. Day was a homely, middle-aged woman, who welcomed him and ushered him into the front parlour.

"Mr. Perry and I are old friends," she said. "I've had his young reporters lodging with me before. I let out one or two rooms and provide breakfast and dinner in the evening. Will that suit you?"

"Yes. That sounds fine," said Edward.

"I'll just show you your room and where the conveniences are," Mrs. Day said as she led Edward upstairs and showed him into a pleasant room overlooking a large back garden.

He had just enough time to grab a pint and a pie in a nearby pub before reporting back to Mr. Perry.

John Perry read through Edward's first report and looked at him.

"Who else was there besides the coffin, the vicar and the widow? No bevy of grieving relatives? No floral tributes? It's a bloody good job I know who was being buried."

"I did notice that the widow nipped off rather quickly with some bloke in a flashy car."

"That'll be the solicitor. Poor old Joe; not cold in his grave and she's off to find out how much he left her."

"Shall I set that up for the front page Mr. Perry?" George sniggered.

John Perry's look would have frozen the ink on the press.

"How did your first day go, Mr. Lewis?" asked Mrs. Day of a rather subdued Edward.

"Not bad. Not bad, all things considered," sighed Edward, as he tucked into the plateful of lamb hotpot that Mrs. Day placed before him.

Before his next assignment, Edward made a few notes of his own. Get the names right; especially the initials. There seemed to be an awful lot of people with the same surname in this small town. If possible go and make a recce of the venue beforehand.

How was he supposed to know that the Women's Institute met in the Elmersdale Memorial Hall and not the church hall? Make a note of any local businesses involved. Why hadn't he made a note of the undertaker's name at that disastrous funeral? There were only two of them in the town and he had managed to name the wrong one. He was to learn that keeping your pencils sharpened was a good idea, when his fountain pen ran out of ink at a crucial moment in a town council meeting.

"Like the theatre do you?" John Perry asked Edward.

"Yes."

"Right then. The Elmersdale Dramatic Society are doing their adaption of 'Hay Fever' by Noel Coward. Go along to the dress rehearsal and make a few notes and then go to the opening night on Friday and do a review."

Fortified by another of his landlady's substantial dinners, Edward went along to the Memorial Hall on the evening of the dress rehearsal. He crept in and took a seat at the back of the hall, notebook at the ready, pencils sharpened. Everything seemed to be going along swimmingly, until the leading lady tripped as she came through the French windows and went headlong into the back of the settee on stage. Members of the cast rushed to her aid and she was assisted to a chair.

"Do try not to do that on the night, darling," came a languid voice from the front row.

Edward stiffled a guffaw. The leading lady recovered and the dress rehearsal continued.

Before he left, Edward made a note: 'Buy a programme'. He wasn't going to get caught out again.

Edward's review of 'Hay Fever' passed muster. He put the correct names to the characters they had played. Praised the performances; commented on the authenticity of the costumes and also remembered to give a mention to the electrical shop in the High Street, who had assisted with the stage lighting.

Edward was settling into the life of a cub reporter on the 'Gazette'.

CHAPTER 3

It was at the Manor House Fete some months after he had joined the 'Gazette' that Edward came into contact with Anne Piper. She was helping her mother serve at their farm produce stall and he recognized the pretty girl as the juvenile lead in 'Hay Fever'. He decided to introduce himself on the pretext of writing an article for his paper and in passing said that he had enjoyed her performance in the play.

Anne smiled at him and thanked him, then she said, "Why don't you come along to our next meeting? We're doing the 'Pirates of Penzance' and we're a bit short of pirates."

Edward said he would think about it.

He and Anne met on several occasions afterwards, not quite by chance. On market days he just happened to be on an errand for Mrs. Day to buy items from the farm stall. He went along to report on the Young Farmers' Annual Dance and was invited to join Anne and the group of people she was with to make up a set for 'Sir Roger de Coverley' and acquitted himself quite well, considering he really hadn't a clue what the dance was all about.

He liked Anne's friends and they accepted him, albeit a little warily, as he accompanied Anne to the buffet table in the interval. Finally Edward plucked up courage and asked Anne to go and watch a film with him at the little town's one cinema.

They arranged to meet outside the cinema in time to park their bicycles side by side, before going in for the performance. Edward decided to splash out and the usherette showed them to their seats in the one and nines. The programme began with a short travelogue followed by the Pathe Gazette News. The safety curtain was lowered and the same girl, who had shown them to their seats, now came round with a tray carrying sweets, popcorn and a selection of ice creams.

Anne said she would like a choc-ice and they sat companionably eating their ice creams until the safety curtain rose and the big film began.

It was an Agatha Christie thriller and in a tense moment Edward took hold of Anne's hand and squeezed it reassuringly. She hid her face in his shoulder until he said, "It's all right. You can look now." But he still kept hold of her hand.

At the end of the film they stood up while the National Anthem was played and then went outside to collect their bicycles. They rode back to 'Piper's Farm' discussing the film.

"I would never have guessed it was that doctor," said Anne.

"Well, it isn't always the butler."

"I bet you didn't guess either."

"No I didn't. I thought it was the son."

"But he was murdered too."

"No, not that one. The other son; the artist."

"Oh, I liked him."

"Did you? I thought he had the most to gain."

"Yes, but I still felt a bit sorry for the doctor."

They had reached the farm gate and Edward got off his bike to open it and he and Anne walked the rest of the way up to the farmhouse door. Anne thanked Edward for a lovely evening and he said, "Perhaps we could go next week."

"Yes, I'd like that."

Edward cycled back to his lodgings, where Mrs. Day was waiting with a cup of cocoa and some digestive biscuits.

Edward took his cocoa and biscuits up to his room and as he got ready for bed, he mulled over the evening.

'Anne Piper was a really nice girl. So straightforward and uncomplicated and she was very pretty too. I could fall for her,' he thought, before he drifted off to sleep.

Edward became a regular visitor to 'Piper's Farm'. He got on well with Mr. and Mrs. Piper and was often invited back to supper after church on Sunday. He and Sam Piper would discuss farming matters and Edward sought his advice about setting up a regular column in the 'Gazette' dealing with such matters.

CHAPTER 4

Life meandered along pleasantly in Elmersdale, but abroad in the country the sense of unease at the rise of the German Chancellor, Adolf Hitler, and his Nazi Party persisted. People spoke of peace, but thought of war. Any scrap of optimism was seized upon and when the Prime Minister, Mr. Neville Chamberlain, went to Munich in September 1938, for a meeting with Herr Hitler, he felt his first duty was to avoid plunging his country into war at all costs.

Listening to the wireless, reading the newspaper articles, watching the newsreels at the cinema, the general public was relieved that for the time being the crisis had been held at bay. Hadn't the Prime Minister guaranteed 'peace in our time'?

Edward sometimes managed to get the odd weekend off, when he went back home to see his parents. He amused his mother with tales of the 'goings-on' in Elmersdale and picked his father's brain. He was also able to meet his friends and keep up-to-date with what was going on in the world outside Elmersdale.

Cycling back to the farm after one of their weekly visits to the cinema, Anne said, "Do you think there will be a war Edward?"

He had been home the previous weekend and had been talking to his father about Mr. Chamberlain's meeting with Herr Hitler. His father was sceptical about this act of appeasement.

"I really don't know," he replied.

In April 1939 Mr. Chamberlain announced conscription for young men of twenty and twenty-one years of age, and on his next weekend home Edward and some of his university friends went into a recruiting centre and volunteered for the army.

"Like the 'Pals' Brigade' in the First War," his father said when Edward told him what they had done.

His mother lost all of the colour from her face and poured herself a glass of sherry.

War was declared between Great Britain and Germany on Sunday, September 3rd 1939 and one morning, shortly afterwards, the postman knocked on Mrs. Day's door and said that there was an official letter for Mr. Lewis 'to be signed for'. Edward knew by the look of the envelope that it contained his calling-up papers.

He went straight to the Editor's office when he went into work that morning. John Perry was not all that surprised at Edward's news and asked him when he expected to leave.

"I've got my medical next week."

Mr. Perry nodded and gave him his list of assignments.

Later that same day, Edward cycled up to 'Piper's Farm'. Anne opened the door and said, "Edward. I wasn't expecting you. Come in."

"No. Have you got a minute?"

"Is everything all right?"

"Yes. I just need to talk to you."

"Come and help me put the chickens to bed."

Edward followed Anne round to the poultry enclosure and leaned against the fence.

"I've got my calling-up papers. I've to go for my medical next week."

"Oh dear. What will happen then?"

"Well, I expect if I pass, I'll be called up for basic training."

Anne shivered, although the September evening was balmy.

"I've arranged it with Mr. Perry to go home for a few days next week, but we could still go to the flicks on Saturday."

"All right."

"Meet you as usual then?"

"Yes."

Edward cycled off and Anne went back inside the farmhouse to break the news to her parents.

Edward had his medical and the time came for him to say "goodbye" to Elmersdale. Mrs. Day wept copious tears. John Perry shook his hand, said he was sorry to lose him and wished him luck. George, the one time office boy, now reporter second class, slapped him on the back and said he expected that he would soon be getting his calling-up papers; knowing that he probably wouldn't be classed A1, due to his poor eyesight and flat feet.

Edward went to 'Piper's Farm' to say goodbye to Mr. and Mrs. Piper and to thank them for their kindness to him while he had lived in Elmersdale. Anne walked with him to the farm gate. He turned her towards him and held her close. On an impulse he said, "Will you marry me Anne?"

Anne hesitated. She wasn't expecting a proposal of marriage; then she looked up into Edward's face and what she saw there made her heart begin to beat faster.

"Will you, Anne? Will you marry me?" he said again.

"Yes," she said, smiling up at him. "Yes, I will."

He bent his head to kiss her and shyly, at first, she kissed him back.

"I'll write to let you know where I am and when I get leave you must come to London and meet my parents."

"All right."

He kissed her again and she put her arms around him and held him tight.

"Goodbye sweetheart."

"Goodbye Edward. Take care. Write to me soon."

They kissed each other goodbye and then kissed again.

"I love you," he said and blew her a kiss as he mounted his bike.

"I love you," she called after him and swallowed hard as she watched him cycle away, her eyes bright with unshed tears.

CHAPTER 5

Private Edward Lewis completed his basic training course and was granted the customary leave. However, before he went on leave, he was summoned to his Commanding Officer's office. He racked his brains to think what he could have done. He hoped it wasn't too serious and that it would mean his leave was cancelled. He touched the breast pocket of his battle-dress jacket. He had his pass and his travel docket. He had arranged for Anne to come up to London that weekend to meet his parents.

'Oh Lord,' he thought. 'Here I am sitting in the outer office again waiting to be interviewed.'

He was marched into the CO's office by the Lance Corporal. He saluted smartly and on being invited to sit down, removed his forage cap. The CO was looking at Edward's report sheet.

"I see you were a journalist in civvy street, Lewis?"

"Yes sir." Edward didn't elaborate on his journalistic prowess.

"We think you could be useful to us in the Intelligence Corps."

"Sir?"

"Report for officer training when you get back from leave."

Edward stood up, put his cap back on and, returning his CO's sketchy salute, marched out.

He just made it onto the truck taking those going on leave to the station. The train was crowded with service personnel and he stood most of the way home.

He turned his key in the lock and opened the door to the familiar smell of home. His mother came hurrying from the back of the house.

"Edward, you're home," she said, as she hugged and kissed him.

"Steady on Mum. I've only been gone eight weeks."

"I know, but it's so lovely to have you back safe and sound." And she hugged and kissed him again.

"I could do with a cup of tea, Mum."

"Yes, of course you could. Have you had anything to eat? Your father won't be home until later. I expect you could do with a sandwich or something."

They sat at the kitchen table and his mother watched as he drank his tea and demolished her cheese ration in a sandwich, but she didn't care. He was home, if only for a few days. She was nervous too. Edward had written to his parents telling them that he had asked Anne Piper to marry him and tomorrow she would be coming to stay for the weekend.

Over dinner that evening he told his parents about his interview with his Commanding Officer.

"What do you think I should do, Dad? I had hoped to be posted to a unit with some of the chaps I've met."

"Does it mean you won't be sent overseas?" his mother said. She felt that if only he could stay in England, he would be safe. She remembered her elder brother, the same age as Edward was now, going to fight in France in the First World War and the devastating effect it had had on her mother when he had been killed at Passchendaele in 1917.

Frank Lewis caught his wife's eye and shook his head imperceptibly.

"It might be interesting. You would be gaining experience that could be useful to you when this is all over."

"You think I should go for it then, Dad?"

"Yes. I do."

His mother smiled at Edward and said, "I expect you're tired. Have a nice hot bath and I'll come in and see you later. You can have my six inches of water as well."

Edward smiled at his mother's little joke.

When he had left the room, Ellen Lewis turned to her husband.

"I couldn't bear it if anything happened to him," she said.

"Yes we could," he replied. "But it won't. Come on. I've a busy day tomorrow and you have to prepare for the girlfriend."

"Yes. She sounds nice though, doesn't she?"

Ellen Lewis stood looking down at her sleeping son and her heart contracted. This time he wasn't going to university, or even going to Elmersdale. This time he was going off to war.

Chapter 6

Edward was up bright and early on Saturday morning and had breakfast with his mother. He was meeting Anne's train at eleven o'clock.

"You'll like her Mum," he said as he prepared to leave.

Ellen nodded. "Off you go then. You don't want to keep her waiting."

She waved Edward off, closed the door and went into the kitchen to wash the breakfast dishes before going upstairs to prepare the spare room for Anne.

Edward took the underground to Victoria Station and as he sat down an advert for Bravington's caught his eye.

'I'll give you a ring,' a young man was speaking into a telephone. On the other end of the line a young woman had a vision of a diamond solitaire. He hadn't bought Anne a ring yet. 'We'll choose it today before we go home,' he decided.

Edward waited impatiently behind the barrier as Anne's train drew in. She stepped down from the carriage and began to walk towards the ticket collector, hastening her step, her face breaking into a smile as she saw him waiting for her.

"Hello," he said.

"Hello. You look very smart."

It was the first time Anne had seen Edward in uniform.

"You look beautiful."

He took hold of her small suitcase and as they left the station arm in arm, Edward said, "There's something we must do before I take you to meet Mum and Dad."

He had noticed a jeweller's shop just around the corner from the station and had stopped to look at the trays of rings in the window before going to meet Anne. He was sure she would find something there she liked. As they reached the shop, Anne looked up at him.

"Edward?" she queried.

"Let's make it official, shall we?" he said and ushered her in.

A bell over the door made the shopkeeper aware that he had prospective customers and he came from the back of the shop and smiled at them.

"We'd like to see some engagement rings, please," said Edward.

"Yes sir. Certainly sir. Does the young lady have a preference?"

Edward looked at Anne and she shrugged her shoulders slightly.

"Diamonds are always popular."

The jeweller took a key from his waistcoat pocket and went to open one of the doors that closed off the shop-front windows.

He brought back two trays and placed them on the counter. One tray held an assortment of diamond rings and the other a selection of rings with diamonds combined with other precious stones. Edward glanced at the prices and thought that he could probably afford to buy Anne the ring she chose. Anne pointed to a diamond solitaire.

"What do you think Edward?"

"Would madame like to try on the ring?"

Anne held out her left hand and Edward slipped the ring onto her third finger. The diamond caught the light. It was dazzling. And the ring fitted perfectly. Anne looked again at Edward and he smiled back at her and said, "We'll take that one please."

The ring was placed in a dark red leatherette box lined with black velvet and then into a bag with the jeweller's name on it. The jeweller smiled at the happy couple as Edward wrote out a cheque.

"You could have kept it on, you know," Edward said as they came out of the shop.

"I know, but I think I would like to wait until we can show it to your mother and father."

"What would you like to do today?"

"Show me the sights of London. Take me to Trafalgar Square and Piccadilly and Buckingham Palace. Take me to have lunch in a Lyons Corner House."

"Isn't buying you a ring enough, woman? Do you want to bankrupt me? I'm only a poor soldier, you know," he teased her.

Anne laughed. She was so happy to be with Edward again.

Later that day, travelling home together on the underground, Edward pointed out the Bravington's advert to Anne and this combined with the excitement of the day, gave her the giggles.

When they reached Edward's home, he rang the front doorbell. He wanted to give his mother time to compose herself. Ellen Lewis opened the door and saw a slim young woman, who came just up to her son's shoulder. The fresh faced girl smiled at her; a smile that reached her dark brown eyes.

"Come in, my dear," Ellen said. "It's lovely to meet you at last," and turning to Edward said, "Take Anne's case up to the spare bedroom would you please. We'll be in the sitting room," and to Anne she said,"Come with me while I put the kettle on. I was just going to make a cup of tea for myself."

Anne followed Ellen into her kitchen and waited while she made a pot of tea and put some biscuits onto a plate and then they both made their way to the sitting room. When Edward came in he found his mother and Anne chatting amiably. He looked at his mother and she smiled at him and said, "Anne and I were just chatting about Elmersdale."

After a while when they had finished drinking their tea, Anne went upstairs to freshen up.

"What do you think of her Mum?" Edward asked his mother. "She's lovely, isn't she?"

"Yes, she is," his mother replied.

Edward knocked on the door of the spare room.

"Anne," he said. "Dad's home. Come down and meet him."

Anne opened the door and beckoned him in.

"Do I look all right?"

He nodded.

She gave Edward the jewellery box and held out her left hand. His fingers trembled as he took the ring out of its box and placed it again on Anne's finger. As he bent to kiss her, she flung her arms about his neck and said, "I do love you so."

He held her close and said, "And I love you, my beautiful girl."

They walked down the stairs together and before they entered the sitting room, Edward took hold of Anne's hand and then led her in to meet his father.

"Dad, this is Anne."

"Hallo Anne. I've heard a lot about you. I gather from Edward we have something to celebrate," Frank Lewis said, as he came towards her smiling a welcome.

Anne smiled shyly at this man who was so like Edward.

"Yes," she said and held out her hand so that he and Edward's mother could see her ring.

Edward put his arm about her waist and held her close and Anne turned to look at him lovingly. Ellen Lewis came to look at the ring.

"It's beautiful my dear," she said. "I wish you well to wear it."

Frank Lewis went over to the drinks table and they all laughed as he popped the cork of the bottle and poured them all a glass of champagne.

"To Edward and Anne," he said and raised his glass in salute.

"To Edward and Anne," his mother echoed.

Anne sipped her first taste of champagne and the bubbles tickled her nose.

"Here," said Frank, handing the cork to Anne. "Keep this for luck."

'How much more luck do I need?' thought Anne and with his arm still around her waist, she followed Edward and his parents into their dining room.

The weekend passed all too quickly. On Saturday evening Edward took her dancing in Covent Garden Opera House, where the auditorium had been converted into a dance hall. 'The Mecca for half the men and girls on leave in Central London' according to a reporter from 'Picture Post'.

On Sunday morning they caught the bus to Highgate Hill and Edward pointed out Dick Whittington's stone, before they went for a walk on Hampstead Heath. It was a fine morning and from the top of Parliament Hill they could see all London spread out before them. They walked down past the ponds, where once children had sailed their toy boats, to the 'Spaniard's Inn'; and Anne didn't know whether to believe Edward or not, when he told her that the notorious highwayman, Dick Turpin, had stopped there on his way to York, escaping from the excise men.

They returned home in time for lunch and in the afternoon those of Edward's friends who also happened to be on leave, dropped in on the off chance of seeing him before going back to their various units. Anne was impressed at the easy manner with which Ellen Lewis coped with all the comings and goings of these young people; serving tea or beer and sandwiches non-stop until they had all gone and there were just the four of them sitting down to a quiet evening listening to the Home Service on the BBC.

Both Anne and Edward had trains to catch on Monday morning; she home to Elmersdale and he to Aldershot to begin his officer training course. Anne thanked Edward's parents for making her so welcome and turned to wave again before getting into the taxi that would take them to the station

Edward bought a platform ticket and went with Anne to find her a seat on the train.

"When I've completed my officer training, I should get some more leave and I'll come down to Elmersdale and talk to your Mum and Dad about our getting married."

Anne nodded. The guard blew his whistle. Edward lifted her hand to his lips and kissed her ring. She stood on tiptoe and kissed him, then boarded the train. Anne stood at the carriage window waving for as long as she could see him standing on the platform waving back.

Edward returned home to collect his gear and say goodbye to his parents before embarking on the next stage of his army career.

CHAPTER 7

It had been three months since Anne had seen Edward, when she went to meet him at Elmersdale Station. As he walked towards her she thought how handsome he looked in his officer's uniform.

"How's my beautiful girl?"

"Still in love with my poor soldier. Come on."

"What's the rush?"

"I came in on the bus, but I've asked Fred if he will give us a lift back to the farm in his van. He's delivering some feed for Mum's chickens and won't take kindly to being kept waiting."

"Aren't I staying with Mrs. Day then?"

"No. She's got two evacuees billeted on her. You can go and see her later. You're staying with us on the farm."

They hurried out of the station to find Fred waiting for them.

"Morning Fred," said Edward.

"Morning Mr. Lewis. I've put a sack on the front seat. Don't want to get muck on that there new uniform, do we?"

"Thanks Fred."

Edward was glad when they got to 'Piper's Farm'. Goodness only knows what had been carried in the van. He was sure people would smell him coming for miles. They got out of the van and Edward collected his hold-all. Anne opened the farm front door and called, "We're home."

Her mother came to meet them.

"Hallo Edward," she said. "My, don't you look smart. Did you have a good journey?"

"Yes, thanks."

"Anne, take Edward into the kitchen and make him a cup of tea, while I go and pay Fred and see that he has taken the chicken feed out to the barn. I'll be back directly to hear all your news."

Edward and Anne grinned at each other and made their way to the farm kitchen, where the Aga gave out a welcoming warmth and a delicious smell of something cooking in it. They sat at the well scrubbed deal table drinking their tea and Anne said, "How long have you got?"

"Only till Monday night. I have to be back in barracks before lights out."

"I've arranged a meeting with Reverend Williams at two o'clock this afternoon to see about reading the banns. Have you brought your birth certificate with you?"

"Yes and my army pay book."

"Will you need that?"

"I don't know. I've never been married before," he said mischievously.

"I expect Reverend Williams will know." She looked up and saw Edward's barely concealed grin.

"Any more jokes like that and I'll have you spud bashing."

"Where on earth did you learn that expression?"

"From listening to you and your friends, when I spent that weekend with your parents."

"I can see I shall have to watch my language."

"Seriously, Edward."

"Yes. Right; down to business. What else have you got planned?"

"I shall have to come back to the farm afterwards to finish my chores, but if you want to go and see Mr. Perry and Mrs. Day, that's fine by me."

At that moment, Mrs. Piper came back into the kitchen.

"That's a good job done," she said. "What time did you say you were going to see the vicar?"

"Two o'clock," said Anne.

Her mother looked at the grandfather clock standing in a corner of the kitchen.

"We'd better get on with lunch then. Soup and bread and cheese I think. Will that suit you Edward?"

"Yes, that's fine." he replied, remembering the taste of homemade soup, home baked bread and farmhouse cheese with relish. He wondered if there was still some of Mrs. Piper's apple chutney left in her store cupboard.

As they cycled along the lanes leading into Elmersdale the trees and hedgerows were beginning to show a green haze and wild violets and primroses were already scenting the air.

"Do you know, I hadn't realised how much I missed all this," Edward said, breathing deeply.

The vicar of St. Philip the Evangelist was waiting for them in the vestry. Edward had attended the church regularly during his stay in Elmersdale and Anne had been the first baby the vicar had baptised, when he had come to the church as a young curate.

"Good afternoon Anne. Nice to see you again, Edward. How's life treating you these days?" he said and shook hands with them.

"Come and sit down and we'll get on with the paperwork. Any idea of when the happy day will be?"

"Not really," said Anne. "It all depends on when Edward gets his next leave."

"Well, as long as you can give me some idea nearer the time, I expect I can fit you in."

He ran his eyes over the details again. "Everything seems to be in order. I'll include the first reading of the banns in my notices on Sunday."

He shook hands again with the young couple and walked with them to the church door.

"I'll be getting back then," Anne said, as they passed through the lych gate. "We usually eat about seven o'clock on Saturday. Mum does 'high-tea', so that will give you plenty of time to catch up on all the gossip with Mrs. Day and have a pint with Mr. Perry. 'Bye," and giving Edward a quick peck on his cheek she cycled off back to the farm.

Edward decided he would call in at the 'Gazette' office first and see how things were since he had been away. He found the office much the same as he had left it. The smell of John Perry's pipe still hung in the air and George's table was as untidy as ever. Edward knocked on the door of the Editor's office and in answer to John Perry's gruff "Come," he went in.

"Hello Edward. I'd heard you were in town."

He came from behind his desk to shake Edward's hand.

"The old grapevine's still working then."

"Yes. I met Fred on the way to the station this morning and he told me he was going to give you and Anne a lift to the farm. What are you up to these days?"

Edward filled him in on what had happened to him since leaving Elmersdale and his purpose for spending his weekend leave with Anne. Noticing his absence, Edward said, "How's George? What's he doing these days? Has he been called up?"

"No. Much to his disappointment, he failed his medical. He runs the local ARP station down in the church hall in his spare time. He gets a bit of stick about enforcing the black-out, but he takes it in good part. He's joined the observer corps and is becoming quite a dab hand with his camera as well."

"Good for him. Doing any special features in the paper?"

"Not really. There's not a lot worth reporting lately. All the usual stuff. New regulations from the Ministry of Agriculture. My wife does a special recipe each week on making the best of your rations. The WI give notice of the 'Make Do and Mend' classes they run in the Memorial Hall. That kind of thing."

Edward looked at his watch. "I want to drop in on Mrs. Day to see how she is. Are you going to the 'Black Bull' before you go home this evening?"

"Yes."

"OK then. I'll see you there for a swift half."

Edward parked his bike by the front door of Mrs. Day's house and lifting the lion's head, he knocked. Presently he heard the patter of feet and the door was opened by a solemn faced little girl of about six or seven, sucking her thumb and trailing a rag doll. Edward heard Mrs. Day's voice.

"What have I told you about opening the front door? Oh Mr. Lewis, it's you. I didn't recognise you in that uniform. Come in, I'd heard you were coming down this weekend. How are you? Close the door Lily."

She took hold of the child's hand and led the way into the back kitchen and Edward followed her.

"I'll put the kettle on."

She bustled about laying out cups and saucers, found a doyley and some plates and took a cake out of a tin.

"There we are then. Now tell me all about what you've been doing since you left Elmersdale."

"Anne said that you had two evacuees," Edward said, as they sat drinking their tea and eating slices of fruit cake.

"Yes. Lily is the little one. The elder girl, Rose, has gone to play with a friend who is billeted in the next street. They all come from the same school in London. It's putting a bit of a strain on the local school. Our children go to school in the morning and the evacuees go in the afternoon. It can't go on like this. Something will have to be done. Mind you they do have their own teachers. There is talk of putting them in the old church school. Another cup of tea?"

"Yes please."

Edward spent a pleasant hour chatting with Mrs. Day; listening to all the Elmersdale gossip. How the colonel had come out of retirement to run the Local Defence Volunteers and his wife, Lady Brewster, had formed a branch of the Women's Voluntary Service and had enlisted most of the members of the Women's Institute.

"Have you joined the WVS?"

"Yes."

"What do you do?"

"We knit 'comforts' for the services on what used to be our arts and crafts afternoon and we work a rota to run a mobile canteen for the army camp that's been built on some land bordering on the grounds of the Manor House and Oakwood Farm. Commandeered by the government it was. The Colonel didn't say much, but old Harry Oakwood was none too pleased I can tell you."

Edward answered Mrs. Day's questions about what had been happening to him since he had joined up and why he had come down to Elmersdale this weekend.

"I have to go now, Mrs. Day. I said I would meet Mr. Perry for a drink before I make my way back to the farm. Thanks for the tea and your fruit cake is still the best."

Mrs. Day saw him to the door and said he was to be sure to come and see her the next time he was in Elmersdale.

"I'll send you an invitation to the wedding."

"I should think so," his landlady said as she waved him off.

After supper that evening Anne said, "Go into the parlour. There's today's paper and some farming magazines. I'll just give Mum a hand with the dishes and then when Dad comes in from his rounds, I'll make some tea. Turn the wireless on if you like and put a few more logs on the fire."

Edward went into the parlour and crossed over to the big bay window and looked out. It was getting dusk and a crescent moon was just rising. The countryside beyond the farm and the farmyard itself took on a peaceful air, so different from the turmoil going on in the rest of Europe. He turned and went over to the old upright piano and lifted the lid. He sat down on the long piano stool and ran his fingers over the keys. It somehow seemed appropriate to play 'Sheep May Safely Graze' and then he played a Chopin Nocturne that was a favourite of his mother's.

Anne came quietly into the room and stood watching him play, until sensing her presence Edward turned and smiled at her.

"I didn't know you played the piano."

"Ah, there are a lot of things you don't know about me."

"Why have you never played before?"

"Well, I wasn't engaged to the daughter of the house then and besides your Dad usually cornered me for a chat about farming. Do you play?"

"Yes I do."

"Come and sit down beside me."

Edward began to play some of the popular tunes of the day; improvising and jazzing them up.

"Who taught you to play like that?"

"The school I went to had a pretty good music department and then when I went to university, some of the chaps formed a jazz band. Who taught you to play?"

"Mrs. Williams."

"What, the vicar's wife?"

"Mm. Yes. She was a local girl who came back to teach in Elmersdale and she was the deputy church organist. That's how she and Mr. Williams met and after they were married, she gave piano lessons to help out financially."

"Why have I never heard you play?"

"Ah, there are a lot of things you don't know about me," she teased him.

He looked at her sweet face.

"I know that I love you," he said.

"And I know that I love you," she replied, as he took her in his arms and kissed her.

On Sunday morning Edward and Anne went to church to hear the Reverend Williams read the banns of the intended marriage between Anne Louise Piper, spinster of this parish, and Edward Philip Lewis, bachelor of the parish of St. Mary, Islington, London, for the first time.

As they left the church, members of the congregation came to congratulate them. Anne proudly showed the women her diamond engagement ring and the men shook Edward's hand and told him he was a lucky fellow. Finally they managed to escape and make their way back to the farm.

The rest of the day was spent quietly. There were still jobs to be done around the farm and Edward lent a hand where he was able. In the evening, the talk turned to the war and what was happening in France. Sam Piper was losing Tom, his young farm hand, to the armed forces and there was talk of young girls joining a Women's Land Army.

"Of course," said Mr. Piper, "women have always worked on farms, but they were farmers' wives and daughters, not city girls."

Farmers are early risers, so after listening to the nine o'clock news, Anne's parents wished them goodnight and went up to bed, leaving the young couple time to themselves. Anne's mother turned before she left the room and said to Edward, "Don't keep her up too late. She has an early start in the morning."

"I won't," he promised.

They sat on the large comfortable sofa and Edward put his arm around Anne's shoulder and she nestled into him, making plans – between kisses – for their wedding, until the clock ticking away on the mantelshelf began to strike eleven o'clock.

"Come on, sweetheart, I promised your mother I wouldn't keep you up late."

They went upstairs together and parted with a goodnight kiss before going to their separate rooms.

Edward was catching an early train out of Elmersdale on Monday morning and wanted to be up in good time to say goodbye to Mr. and Mrs. Piper. As he came downstairs the inviting smell of frying bacon reached his nostrils. He put his hold-all in the hall and went into the kitchen, where Mrs. Piper was standing at the Aga tending the frying pan. She turned as Edward came in.

"Good morning Edward. Did you sleep well?"

"Yes thanks."

"I thought you could do with a good breakfast inside you. You don't know how long it will be before you eat again. Anne and her father have gone to the milking parlour, but you sit down and make a start. They'll be here directly."

And with that she put a plateful of bacon and eggs in front of him, cut him a slice of home baked bread spread thickly with butter and poured him a cup of tea.

She sat down with him at the table, drinking her own tea and watched him enjoying his breakfast. She liked Edward and felt Anne would be happy married to him.

Mr. Piper and Anne came in together, shedding their gumboots and milking overalls in the lobby outside the back door. Sam Piper rubbed his hands.

"It's a mite chilly out there this morning," he said and went over to the kitchen sink to wash his hands before sitting down at the table to begin his breakfast.

"All set then, lad?"

Edward nodded.

Anne had once more enlisted the services of Fred, so that she could go to the station with Edward. This gave her the added advantage of being able to put her bike in the back of the van and cycle back to the farm after seeing him off. She spoke to Edward as she stood washing her hands.

"Fred said he would be here by half past seven, so that should get us to the station in good time."

She sat down beside him and poured herself a cup of tea.

"Aren't you having any breakfast Anne?" her mother asked.

"No. I'm not very hungry just now," she replied, because the lump in her throat made swallowing difficult.

The sound of Fred's motor horn startled her. Goodbyes were said quickly and Edward collected his bag and followed Anne out to Fred's van. He put her bike in first, then slung his hold-all in after it. They both turned to wave again to Anne's parents, standing at the farm door, then Fred started up the engine and they were away.

At the station, Edward took out his bag and Anne's bicycle, which he propped up against the station fence. He shook hands with Fred and thanked him for driving them to the station.

"Next time I see you, I'll fetch the limousine and take you to the church," Fred joked. "Safe journey Mr. Lewis. God bless you."

Anne and Edward were left standing on the platform in the cold morning air, holding hands tightly, awaiting the train that would take them away from each other. Neither of them said much.

"Here she comes," said Anne, as the whistle and the plume of smoke alerted them to the train's arrival.

Edward kissed her fiercely and she clung to him.

"Don't you go making eyes at those soldiers up at the camp," he joked lamely.

"As if I would."

Edward kissed her again and boarded the train. He leant out of the carriage window and she came to him and reached up to kiss him again.

Edward stood at the carriage window and waved for as long as he could see Anne waving back and experienced a sense of déjà vu.

CHAPTER 8

Ellen Lewis stood at the barrier waiting for Edward's train to arrive. She was glad that he had caught an early train and that she would be able to spend a little time with him before he left again. She saw him alight from the train and her heart lifted at the sight of her handsome boy. She waved.

Edward saw his mother waiting for him and waved and smiled as he hurried along the platform to meet her.

"I thought we could take a taxi to Dad's office. Miss Prior will probably be able to make us some coffee while we wait for your father to settle the paper and then we can all go to lunch together," his mother said.

Edward hailed a taxi and as they drove away Ellen said, "Now tell me all about your weekend. How was Anne? And her parents? Did you see the vicar about reading the banns? Did you manage to see John Perry and Mrs. Day?"

She knew she was talking too much. Hardly giving him time to answer one question before she asked another. Edward took hold of his mother's hand and stroked it, calming her and answering her questions and asking how things were with her and his father, until by the time they reached Fleet Street, she was her usual self.

Over lunch at the Strand Palace Hotel, Edward brought his father up–to-date with his latest posting at MI5 and they talked about the war in general, until his mother interrupted and said she had had enough of war talk and wanted to know more about the wedding plans and if he had asked Anne what she would like as a wedding present. From then on the conversation took on a lighter tone, until his father took out his pocket watch and said it was time he was going back to his office.

Outside the hotel, Edward and his father shook hands and Frank Lewis kissed his wife's cheek and said he shouldn't be too late home that evening and set off at a brisk pace towards Fleet Street. Ellen looked after her husband and gave a slight shrug of her shoulders.

"Is he working too hard?" enquired Edward.

"Yes, but then he always has," his mother said.

She slipped her arm through Edward's and said, "It's a lovely afternoon. Let's walk for a while before we catch the bus to the station.

"Tell me about Woodstock," Ellen said later, as they stood on the platform waiting for Edward's train.

"Well, it's rather a quaint little country town, quite close to Bladon, where I'm based. Malvern College is in fact a school in the grounds of Blenheim Palace."

Ellen touched her son's arm. "On second thoughts, should you be telling me this Edward? Careless talk and all that."

Edward laughed and said that far from being a secret location, the local bus conductors, on reaching the Blenheim Palace gates, would call out, "Anyone for MI5?"

His mother looked at him in disbelief and then burst out laughing.

So Edward boarded the train to Woodstock and the machinations of MI5, and his mother caught a bus back to Islington and an empty house.

Chapter 9

Anne's first thought when she woke each morning was, 'Would that all important letter from Edward, saying when his next leave would be, arrive today?'

The war was not going well for the Allies. The fall of France and the Low Countries and the retreat of the British Expeditionary Force made her thankful that, at least, in Oxford, Edward was as safe as he could be in wartime; but who knew where he would be posted to in the future?

Her mother, ever practical, encouraged her to begin preparations for her wedding. She brought her own wedding dress down from the big trunk in the attic, unpacked it from the layers of tissue paper and shook out the creases.

"Come and try this on Anne," she said.

Anne looked at the dress. She was taller than her mother and slimmer and it was not quite what she had hoped for. Still it was wartime.

"Hmm," her mother said. "Perhaps if we take it to Etherington's in the High Street, Miss Etherington might have some material in the back of the shop that would make it a bit more fashionable. We'll go into town tomorrow afternoon."

And she returned the dress to its box.

That night, as she lay in bed, Anne was torn between hurting her mother's feelings and hoping that Miss Etherington would not come up with any bright ideas.

They caught the bus into Elmersdale on Monday afternoon, carrying the dress in its old-fashioned box, and made their way to the small department store in the High Street.

Miss Etherington of Etherington & Son – High Class Draper – smiled as she saw Mrs. Piper and Anne enter the shop.

"Good afternoon Mrs. Piper. Anne. What can I do for you?"

"Good afternoon Miss Etherington. As you know, Anne is shortly to be married to Mr. Lewis. You know, he used to be a reporter on the 'Gazette'."

Peggy Etherington remembered Edward Lewis as a very pleasant young man.

"He's an officer in the army now," Nancy Piper went on.

"Yes, I saw him in town not so long ago. He looked very handsome in his uniform." She smiled again at Anne.

"We wondered if you would have any ideas to bring my wedding dress up-to-date?"

Peggy Etherington glanced quickly at the box and then at Anne's face. She remembered selling that dress to Nancy Davies, as she then was, all of twenty-five years ago.

"Come into the office and we'll have a look, shall we?" and she led the way into a small room at the back of the shop, put the box on the cutting table and opened it. She shook out the dress and held it up.

"The fabric is very delicate and it is such a lovely dress. It would be a pity to spoil it by trying to unpick it and perhaps ruin it. Trying to add a different material isn't always successful." She sowed the seeds of doubt in Nancy Piper's mind and the seeds of hope into Anne's.

"What do you suggest then?"

"Do you still have your veil, Mrs. Piper?"

"Yes. It's in the box somewhere."

"We have some very pretty dresses in the Bridal Department at the moment and they are quite reasonable. Would you like to come and look? Something old, something new," she said.

Anne watched as Miss Etherington ran her hands over a rack of bridal gowns until she came to one and released it from its cellophane wrapping. She held it up against Anne's slim figure.

"I think your veil would go well with this dress, Mrs. Piper. Try the dress on, Anne, and I'll go and get some pins."

Anne went into the dressing cubicle and tried on the dress. She looked in the long mirror and saw herself walking up the aisle on her father's arm to meet Edward. She came out of the cubicle to see what her mother thought of the dress. Nancy Piper looked at her daughter and thought, 'What is it about a wedding dress that makes a pretty girl beautiful?'

She said, "Very nice dear."

"Before you decide," said Miss Etherington, "try this one."

Anne went back to try the second dress. She liked this one even better.

"What do you think Mum? This one or the first one?"

"I don't know. What do you think Miss Etherington?"

"They are both very beautiful, but I think this one suits you better. The material hangs so well and emphasises your slim waist and the detail of the buttoned sleeves and the sweetheart neckline is so fashionable."

She picked up the veil and draped it over Anne's head and fixed it in place with the pins.

"Your veil does complement this dress beautifully, don't you think? And, as I said," – she showed the price tag to Anne's mother – "very reasonably priced."

Mrs. Piper was pleasantly surprised.

"We'll take it," she said.

Anne kissed her mother's cheek. "Thanks Mum. I think your veil is just so lovely."

Anne smiled her thanks to Miss Etherington, who smiled back. 'Anne was a sweet girl,' she thought. 'She deserves a new wedding dress.'

"Is there anything else I can help you with?" she asked, as she wrapped the dress in layers of tissue paper and packed it in its box.

"Not for the moment, thank you," Mrs. Piper said, as she settled the bill, "but I dare say there will be other things nearer to the day."

"Are you going to have bridesmaids?"

"I don't know. Perhaps Cousin Eileen, Mum?"

"Yes, perhaps."

Eileen was her sister Elsie's daughter, and Nancy knew that it would please them both if Anne asked her to be her bridesmaid. The girls had always got on well together.

"Come along Anne, or we'll miss the bus."

Sitting on the bus on their journey home, mother and daughter had very different thoughts. Anne was so glad that Miss Etherington had persuaded her mother to buy her a new wedding dress. She did so want to look beautiful for Edward. And she was right about the veil. It had made all the difference.

'Miss Etherington must have been very pretty once,' she thought. 'I wonder why she never married?'

Nancy Piper was remembering the day when Peggy Etherington had picked out a wedding dress for her. She had looked very wistfully at Nancy, so happy to be marrying Sam Piper, since her own hopes of happiness had been dashed when her young man had been killed at Ypres in 1915. And she was right; her wedding dress was too delicate and held so many lovely memories of the day she and Sam had been married for it to be cut about and altered. Had she looked as lovely in her wedding dress as Anne had today, she wondered?

CHAPTER 10

Anne came into the kitchen carrying a batch of letters. Sifting through them quickly, she found the one from Edward and sat down at the table to read it. She handed the rest to her father.

"All smiles this morning are we? I hope it's better news than this load of rubbish. More restrictions from the Ministry. How am I expected to run a farm and cope with this lot?"

"I'll give you a hand with them later, Dad."

Anne opened Edward's letter and read it through quickly, hoping it would say what she wanted to hear.

"He's got leave. Edward's got leave. He'll be coming on the last Saturday in July."

Her mother came over and stood behind Anne to read the letter.

"That means it will have to be a Sunday wedding."

She went over to the calendar and counted the Sundays. It was mid June now.

"Just as well we made an early start. It doesn't leave us much time. About five weeks by my reckoning."

"Have you finished your breakfast Anne?" her father said. "It's time we were making a start."

Anne tucked Edward's letter behind the clock on the mantelshelf and went to help her father turn the cows out to pasture.

When they had gone, Nancy Piper's thoughts returned to preparations for the wedding. Anne was meeting Eileen in Elmersdale this Saturday morning and they were going to Etherington's to buy her bridesmaid's dress. Now that they had a better idea of when the wedding might be they could go to the florist and order Anne's bouquet and Eileen's posy. They could also call in at the vicarage on their way home and let Mr. Williams know, so that he could fit the wedding ceremony into his Sunday schedule. She had already made the wedding cake; only one tier and not as fruity as she would have liked, but that couldn't be helped, what with everything being rationed. They were lucky that one of her WI friends was the baker's wife and she had volunteered to ice it. That just left the wedding breakfast. Most of the food would come from the farm and her sister, Elsie, had said she would give her a hand on the morning of the wedding to lay out the buffet in the dining room. She hoped it would be a fine day, then some of the guests could spill out into the garden just outside the dining room. Besides her many accomplishments, Nancy Piper was a keen gardener and, weather permitting, her garden would be looking its best.

"Thank goodness I only had Anne," she said out loud to herself. "I need a cup of tea."

That evening after supper, the wedding list was brought out. Sam Piper groaned and took himself off into the parlour to read the paper and Anne and her mother sat at the kitchen table and went through the arrangements.

"I think now that we have a definite date, you should write to Edward's parents and ask them to send you a list of the guests they would like to invite."

"Yes, I'll do that right now and when I go to see Mr. Williams I'll see Mrs. Williams too and ask her to suggest some music. It's a pity that the church bells can't be rung, but we can't have everyone thinking we are being invaded. Perhaps the choir could sing something. What do you think?"

"Ask Mrs. Williams. She's good at that sort of thing. When you have finished your letter, would you make the cocoa, please? I'm going to listen to the news."

Ellen Lewis was pleased to get Anne's letter asking her to send their guest list, but beside that, Anne had written telling them about buying her wedding dress and that she was going to wear her mother's veil.

"That's something old, something new," she said to her husband when she gave him the letter to read. "I must find something blue to send her."

"Better write to Edward and see if there is anyone he particularly wants to invite. I think we should keep the list short. It's not the easiest place to get to and on a Sunday too," Frank said.

"Yes, I agree. Where do you think we should stay?"

"I'll write to John Perry. He'll know of somewhere."

The guest list enclosed in the reply from Edward's parents was quite short and Nancy Piper breathed a sigh of relief. She didn't want to be overwhelmed by people she didn't know. She reckoned there would be forty all told when their own list was added. As replies to the invitations began to arrive, Nancy checked her list daily.

John Perry's wife had told her at the WI meeting that Edward's parents would be staying with them for the wedding weekend, so she didn't have to worry about that. Mrs. Day had told her that Edward had written to her asking if he and his best man could stay with her. Another problem solved. Some of Edward's friends were coming by train and would go straight to the church and other of his relations – aunts and uncles and cousins – were coming by car. She must remind Fred that they would need two limousines.

She must check that Sam had ordered the firkin of ale from the publican at the 'Black Bull' and if he had asked Harry Oakwood about letting them have a couple of gallons of his cider. She and Sam weren't great drinkers themselves, but no doubt the city folk would want something other than beer and cider. She had better get Sam to buy some sherry as well. And what was it that Anne had had to drink when she and Edward had become engaged? Champagne! She wondered if the publican kept any in stock and made a mental note to ask Sam to enquire the next time he was in town on market day.

The manager of the Co-op had been very helpful and had let her have a couple of packets of tea from his 'emergency' stock, because his daughter and Anne had been at school together and they both belonged to the drama club.

As a farmer's wife, Nancy Piper's life was a busy one, but now it was becoming hectic and there didn't seem to be enough hours in the day and only ten days to go to the wedding.

Chapter 11

Charlie Warburton and Edward had met at university and taken an immediate liking to one another. They had many interests in common, not least their sense of humour and a love of music. They had remained friends, even though their chosen careers had taken different paths when they had obtained their degrees, so it was no surprise when Edward had asked Charlie to be his best man.

Charlie was a 'boffin' and had been seconded from the army to work at some obscure outfit in the country. Many years later, when he and Edward had been swapping war stories, he had told Edward about his work at Bletchley Park and his part in the Enigma decoding operation. He was to spend the night at Edward's parents' home and all four would travel together to Elmersdale on the Saturday before the wedding day.

They arrived at Elmersdale Station and were met by John Perry, who took them home to meet his wife, Sally. After lunch at the Perrys, Edward took Charlie to meet Mrs. Day.

"You'll have to share a room, I'm afraid, Mr. Lewis."

"That's OK Mrs. Day. I can put up with Charlie's snoring for one night."

"My snoring," Charlie said indignantly. "What about you?"

With a parting remark, Mrs. Day left them to hang up their uniforms. "If you want anything ironing, just bring it down to the kitchen."

Charlie raised his eyebrows as Mrs. Day left the room.

"She's a real gem, Charlie," Edward said. "She looked after me really well when I lodged with her. I've got a soft spot for her and she's coming to the wedding too. Get a move on and we might be in time to catch the bus to 'Piper's Farm'; otherwise you'll have to walk there."

"Isn't it bad luck to see the bride before the wedding?"

"Only on the day itself. Besides, it seems ages since I saw Anne and I want to make sure she hasn't changed her mind."

From what Charlie had seen when he had met Anne the weekend she and Edward had become engaged, he very much doubted that.

Charlie had a hard job to keep up with Edward after the bus had dropped them off at the bottom of the lane leading up to the farm. Anne had seen them coming and came flying down the path to be caught up in Edward's embrace.

"Still love your poor soldier then?"

"Yes. Yes. Yes," she said, kissing him between each 'yes'.

"This is Charlie," Edward said. "You remember him? He's going to be my best man."

"Hallo Charlie. Nice to meet you again. Come in and meet my Mum and Dad."

As they made their way to the front door, Edward said, "Before I forget. Mum said to give you this," and he handed her a slim package wrapped in tissue paper.

"What is it?"

"Mum said it was a surprise and you were not to open it until tomorrow."

A pretty young woman, about the same age as Anne, stood in the farm doorway.

"Edward, this is my cousin Eileen. She is going to be my bridesmaid." And to Eileen, "This is Charlie. He's going to be the best man."

Eileen and Charlie eyed each other up and both had the same thought – that this wedding might be more interesting than they had first imagined.

Nancy and Sam Piper were waiting in the farmhouse kitchen to greet their prospective son-in-law and his friend. The table was laid for tea and while they ate, the arrangements for the wedding were discussed, so that Edward could go back and put his parents in the picture.

Walking back down the lane later that evening, after a very satisfying high tea, Charlie said, "They do pretty well in the country, don't they, considering rationing and all that?" And then, "Eileen is quite a pretty girl, isn't she?"

Edward looked sideways at his friend and grinned.

"Come on. Step on it; we're meeting Dad and John Perry for a drink in the 'Black Bull'."

Frank Lewis and John Perry were already in the pub when the two young men arrived, and had been congratulating themselves on the success of Edward's apprenticeship.

"I think Edward will be about ready to join the staff of 'The Chronicle' when this is all over, don't you?"

"God willing," said John Perry. "He's a good lad and has the makings of a fine journalist. Ah. Here they are. What'll you have lads?"

Eileen was sleeping overnight at the farm so that she could be on hand to help her Aunt Nancy and her mother with last minute jobs in the morning, before she helped her cousin dress for her wedding. As they were getting ready for bed she said to Anne, "Charlie is quite good looking, isn't he, Anne?"

"Yes. You'll make a lovely couple," Anne laughed.

"Oh Anne. Honestly. We'd better get our beauty sleep. Goodnight."

"Goodnight. Sleep well. See you in the morning."

Chapter 12

Anne lay in bed listening to the dawn chorus. Today was her wedding day. She looked across at Eileen, who was still asleep. She knew it was far too early to get up, but she was wide awake. She looked out of her bedroom window. Was the sun going to shine on her today? She hoped so and thought of the old adage 'Happy the bride the sun shines upon'. She was happy to be marrying Edward, but these were uncertain times. Would her happiness last?

Having decided to get up anyway, she crept downstairs quietly and was surprised when she went into the kitchen to see her father sitting there drinking tea.

"You're up early," he said.

"I couldn't sleep."

"Neither could I. Big day for you today."

"Yes. Any more tea in the pot?"

Her father poured her a cup and passed it to her and they sat, silently, drinking their tea, each lost in their own thoughts.

Sam Piper remembered the night she had been born. He and Nancy had been married nearly four years and had begun to wonder if they would ever have a child and then Anne had come into their lives. She had been a placid baby; a happy little girl and a carefree young woman, and had brought him much joy. He liked Edward. He was a decent lad and would take good care of their daughter.

Anne was thinking back to her childhood. Her father, kind and patient; never pushing her, but guiding her gently through her life. She could not remember his ever saying a cross word to her.

The grandfather clock striking six broke their reverie.

"Time to bring the cows in," said Anne. "Shall I come with you?"

"No. Go back to bed for a while. Tom will be here presently. We can manage the milking between us."

"It won't be long before he joins up now, will it Dad?"

"No. He's been a good lad. I shall miss him. I'll have a word with him about that young brother of his before he goes. He's leaving school this year, I think, and will be about the same age as Tom was when he first came to work here."

He finished his tea and went towards the back door.

"See you later then," Anne said.

"I'll be ready in good time to take you to the church, my lass," her father replied.

Anne went back upstairs and, much to her surprise, did go back to sleep.

She was wakened the second time by her mother bringing her and Eileen a cup of tea; a rare treat. Eileen stretched sleepily and said, "What time is it?"

"Time you were both up and about. There's a lot to be done this morning," her aunt said. "Drink your tea and then come down and have your breakfast. Your mother will be here soon and I don't want her to find you still in bed."

"I bags the bathroom first," said Eileen.

"OK, but don't take all day."

Anne was glad to have a little time to herself. She looked at her wedding dress hanging on the wardrobe door and felt a shiver of excitement. Today she would become Edward's wife. She leant over and from her bedside table took the package Edward's mother had sent her. She carefully untied the ribbon and folded back the white tissue paper to reveal a white satin garter decorated with a blue silk rose. She smiled. Something old – her mother's veil. Something new – her wedding dress – and now to complete the saying – something blue. Not quite. What was the other thing?

Eileen came into the bedroom swathed in a towel, her newly washed hair wound up in a topknot.

"I hope you're not going to keep it like that," said Anne.

"Of course I'm not. I've brought my curling tongs with me. What do you think of a 'Veronica Lake'?"

Anne rolled her eyes heavenward at Eileen, "You'll make it to the silver screen yet," she said and made her way to the bathroom.

She had been to the hairdresser the day before and if she was careful, her hair would not need much attention and Eileen would give her a hand with arranging it so that the veil and headdress would sit properly.

Both girls came down to breakfast in slacks and blouses. The wedding ceremony wasn't until half past twelve, so there would be ample time to help lay out the buffet before they had to get dressed.

Following the list of instructions Nancy Piper had pinned to the kitchen door, ticking off each task as it was completed, the preparations went relatively smoothly and when her Aunt Elsie had put the finishing touches to her flower arrangements, the dining room looked very bridal. Nancy Piper and her sister and the two girls stood back to admire their handiwork.

"I think that will do, don't you Elsie?"

Anne kissed her mother and her aunt and thanked them. Aunt Elsie patted her arm.

"Now off you go. It's time you two girls were getting dressed. I think we ought to go and get ready too, Nancy. If you get a moment Eileen, just come and give my hair a tweak."

"OK Mum."

Anne and her cousin left their mothers and went upstairs "To make ourselves gorgeous," said Eileen, giggling excitedly.

Edward too had been awake early and waited until he heard Mrs. Day go downstairs before getting up. Putting on his dressing-gown, he went to join her.

"Good morning Mr. Lewis. I didn't think you would be up yet. Is your friend awake?"

"No. Charlie's a sound sleeper. If you're making tea, I'll take him a cup and wake him up."

"Charlie. Wake up. I've brought you a cup of tea."

Charlie stirred himself and said "What time is it, for heaven's sake?"

"Nearly eight o'clock."

"Good Lord man, you're not getting married until half twelve. What on earth are you doing up this early?"

"Country ways, Charlie."

"Give me the city any time," Charlie retorted and made to turn over and go back to sleep.

"Come on Charlie. Drink your tea. By the time we've both had a bath and breakfast, it will be time to walk to Mr. Perry's house.

"Don't they have buses in this part of the country?"

"Not on Sundays. Anyway, the walk will do you good. Blow away the cobwebs."

Charlie sat up and began to drink his tea.

Mrs. Day saw the two young men to the door, clothes-brush in hand, so that they would be 'spick and span' before they left the house. She reached up and kissed Edward on the cheek.

"Good luck Mr. Lewis. I wish you and Anne every happiness."

"Thanks Mrs. Day. See you in church. Goodbye and thanks again for putting me and Charlie up."

"My pleasure. Goodbye Mr. Warburton."

Charlie shook hands with Mrs. Day and thanked her and then he and Edward set off to walk the short distance to John Perry's house, taking their suitcases with them.

Chapter 13

Sam Piper left his farmhand, Tom, to finish the Sunday morning chores and came in to get himself ready to take his daughter to church.

"Sam, the cars are here," Nancy Piper called to her husband.

"Just coming," he said, smoothing down his hair a final time and adjusting his tie yet again.

He came down into the hallway and waited with his wife and sister-in-law at the bottom of the stairs for his daughter and his niece to come down.

"Ready," said Eileen.

"Yes."

"Did you remember to put on the garter Mrs. Lewis gave you?"

"Yes. I'm sure there was something else."

"What?"

"You know. 'Something old, something new'."

"'Something borrowed, something blue'," Eileen finished for her.

"Eileen, I haven't got 'something borrowed'."

"Just a minute."

Eileen went back into the bedroom and came back a few seconds later.

"Here. Tuck this into your garter."

"What is it?"

"It's a lace handkerchief Tom gave me for my birthday."

"Thanks Eileen."

"Are you ready now?"

"Yes."

"You do look lovely," her cousin said admiringly. "You go first and I'll hold your veil up."

"Thanks Eileen. You look lovely too. Charlie won't be able to take his eyes off you."

"Oh, go on with you."

As the two girls came down the stairs, Sam Piper felt a lump come into his throat. His daughter looked so like her mother had on their wedding day. Anne's mother felt her eyes prickle and quickly wiped them with a corner of her handkerchief.

"I'll go with Elsie and Eileen in the first car. Give us five minutes or so and then you and Anne come in the second one."

"Right you are."

Nancy Piper gave her daughter a quick kiss and said, "I'll see you in church then."

Anne returned her mother's kiss and nodded.

At the door, Eileen turned and gave Anne the thumbs up sign. Anne patted the garter and the handkerchief under her wedding dress.

"What are you girls giggling about?" asked Aunt Elsie.

"Nothing Mum."

"Be careful not to crush those flowers as you get into the car."

Father and daughter waited in the hall until the second car arrived at the farm door. Fred in his capacity as chauffeur doffed his cap, opened the limousine door and assisted Anne and Sam into it.

"She's a sight for sore eyes, Sam. As beautiful as they come. That Edward's a lucky fellow."

"That he is," said Sam Piper.

Chapter 14

By the time Edward and his party arrived at St. Philip's Church it was already beginning to fill up with people coming to wish the young couple well. The church flower ladies had arranged an abundance of white blooms at strategic places all around the church and the delicate sweetness of their flowery perfume filled the air. Edward and Charlie sat in the front pew listening to the soothing sound of Mrs. Williams softly playing Edward Elgar's 'Salut D'Amour' on the church organ.

The Reverend Williams came forward to greet Edward and his guests before taking his place in readiness to begin the wedding ceremony. The congregation shuffled expectantly. With a stern frown the minister quelled the choirboys' mischievous grins and at a signal from him, his wife began to play Wagner's 'Bridal Suite' from 'Lohengrin'. Edward and Charlie stood up as Anne and her father began to walk down the aisle towards them. Edward watched entranced as this lovely girl, his Anne, reached his side and turned to hand her bouquet to Eileen, before lifting her veil to smile at him. Charlie patted his pocket to reassure himself that he could produce the ring at the appropriate moment.

The Reverend Williams began the wedding service with the familiar words, "Dearly beloved, we are gathered together, in the sight of God, to marry this man to this woman." Edward and Anne repeated their vows after him and Charlie handed the ring to be blessed, before Edward fitted it onto the third finger of Anne's left hand with the words, "With this ring I thee wed."

While the choir and the congregation sang 'Love divine all love excelling', the vicar led the newly-wed couple and their respective fathers into the vestry to sign the Register.

Mrs. Williams judged the moment to begin to play Mendelssohn's 'Wedding March' from 'A Midsummer Night's Dream' suite as Mr. and Mrs. Edward Lewis walked back into the body of the church and towards the door, through a sea of beaming faces of family and friends. Charlie offered his arm to Eileen and they followed behind the newly-weds. Nancy Piper and Ellen Lewis dabbed their eyes and each took the arm of the other's husband and walked outside to where George was waiting to take the official photos for the 'Elmersdale Gazette'.

The happy couple posed for numerous photographs for the hired photographer from the local studio, before Fred drew up in his limousine to take them back to the farm for the wedding reception. Both sets of parents had been driven back together in the other limousine and arrived in time to greet Edward and Anne and their guests as they arrived at the farm. Charlie and Eileen had crammed into one of Edward's cousin's cars and other guests were ferried to the farm by various other means.

Everybody was in a jolly mood and enjoyed the informality of the occasion. Filling their plates from the generous spread laid out in the dining room, the young people, particularly, enjoyed the novelty of eating out in the garden on such a lovely summer's day; while the older generation found themselves comfortable seats positioned around the dining room, or went into the farm kitchen and sat at the big deal table covered with one of the damask cloths that Nancy and Sam had received as wedding presents.

After the wedding cake had been cut and more photos taken, Anne signalled to Edward that she was going upstairs to change out of her wedding dress. He nodded and went in search of John Perry.

Eileen went upstairs with Anne and after helping her out of her wedding dress, she laid it on Anne's bed. Anne took off the garter and put it away in the drawer of her bedside cabinet. She gave the lace handkerchief back to Eileen and as she changed into her going away outfit, she said to her, "Did I hear you say that Tom, our Tom, gave you that for your birthday?"

"Yes, that's right."

"You're a dark horse. What about Charlie?"

"What about Charlie? I don't suppose I'll see him again and Tom and I have been friends since we were at school together. We've been out a few times and he has asked me to write to him when he goes away to the army."

"And will you?"

"Yes. Be careful how you hang that dress up. I might want to borrow it sometime."

Anne laughed at her cousin, "You cheeky monkey."

Eileen ducked as Anne made to box her ears.

"Are you sure you have packed everything?"

"Yes, I think so."

"Best be getting downstairs then. Mustn't keep Edward from his honeymoon."

After the newly-weds had been driven to the station by John Perry, the wedding guests began to drift away home, thanking Nancy and Sam Piper for a lovely day. Only Edward's parents and Sally Perry remained behind.

While they waited for John Perry to come back from the station Sam Piper showed Frank Lewis round his farm. Their wives retired to the parlour to drink a welcome cup of tea from Nancy's best china. The three women chatted amiably about the wedding and Ellen Lewis said, "It has been a really lovely day. Thank you for making it such a happy occasion for everyone. It must have been a lot of extra work for you."

"It was my pleasure," Nancy replied. "We have grown very fond of Edward and we wanted them to have happy memories of their wedding day."

"It's very peaceful here. I can quite understand why Edward came to love this part of the country."

"If ever the bombing gets too bad, you and Mr. Lewis must come to the farm for a rest," said Nancy.

"That really is most kind of you. So far it has not been too bad. But I fear it may be the lull before the storm."

Sam and Frank came back indoors, bringing John Perry with them. In answer to their questions, he said, "Yes, they caught the train all right. It was just coming into the station as I left."

Frank and Ellen Lewis thanked the Pipers again for a lovely day and Sam and Nancy stood waving them off, as John Perry and his wife drove them away.

"I think everything went off well, don't you Sam?" Nancy said, as she and Sam went back into the farmhouse.

"Yes, very nicely dear, considering one half of the guests had never met the other half before today."

"Edward's parents were really nice folk weren't they? I was a bit nervous about meeting them. I thought your speech went down really well and that young man, Charlie, made us all laugh when he toasted the bride and groom. He and Eileen seemed to get on well together didn't they and it was nice of Mr. Perry to take Anne and Edward to the station."

Sam yawned. "Do you want any help with the clearing up?"

"No. You go and check on the animals. Elsie said she would come and give me a hand in the morning. I don't know about you, but I'm ready for bed. Don't take too long. I'll make us a drink as soon as you come in."

"Right you are. It's been a long day for us both."

And much as he liked Edward, he couldn't help but feel a little sad as he checked on his livestock without his little lass to help him.

Chapter 15

After John Perry left them, Edward picked up their cases and went to the ticket office to buy tickets to Brightbourne. The train drew into the station and Anne and Edward found a carriage to themselves. Edward put his arms around his new wife and kissed her.

"I've got you all to myself for five whole days," he said.

"I know. Isn't it lovely to be going somewhere together, instead of one of us always being left behind?"

They arrived at the small hotel on the South Coast in time for a late dinner. There were only four other people in the dining room; an elderly couple and a young man and a girl about the same age as themselves. As they passed them on their way to their table, Anne noticed particles of confetti clinging to the girl's hair and smiled to herself.

After dinner, Edward collected the key from the reception desk and they went up to their room. The honeymoon had been a gift from Edward's parents and their room was at the front of the hotel and looked out over the sea. It also had its own adjoining bathroom. Anne opened her suitcase and took out her nightgown.

"I'll just…," and she gestured towards the bathroom.

"Yes, of course."

While she was gone, Edward quickly undressed and put on his dressing-gown. He had had a fling with a girl at university, but he suspected that this would be the first time for Anne. He desperately wanted to make love to her, but when she came out of the bathroom she looked so vulnerable that he went to her and, taking her in his arms, said, "It will be all right sweetheart. I promise you it will be all right," before he guided her gently towards the big double bed and turned down the covers.

As she lay in his embrace, he stroked the side of her face and kissed her gently. She felt herself responding to him as he caressed her body and his kisses became more passionate and, surrendering to his love-making, she became Edward's wife.

Anne opened her eyes the next morning to find that Edward was already awake and was leaning on one elbow watching her as she had slept.

"Good morning Mrs. Lewis," he said and kissed her.

"What's the time? Should we be getting up?"

Edward shook his head and drawing her close to him, he made love to her again.

"Are we going to stay in bed all day?"

"If you like."

Anne giggled. "What will people think?"

"All right then. Let's see what's on offer for breakfast."

Due to wartime restrictions and a shortage of staff, there was no room service, so after getting bathed and dressed, they went down to the dining room. The young couple they had seen the evening before were already seated and gave Edward and Anne a self-conscious smile.

"I'll bet they're on honeymoon too," whispered Anne.

"Of course they are. Either that or he's up to no good."

"Edward! How can you say that? Anyway, she had confetti in her hair last night."

Edward waited on the steps of the hotel while Anne went to fetch her handbag. The other young man came and stood alongside him.

"Lovely morning. Hope the weather lasts," he said

"Yes, my wife and I thought we would take a stroll along the front."

"We had the same idea."

"Been married long?" Edward said.

The young man grinned at him. "Yesterday. You?"

Edward grinned back. "Me too."

They were joined by their wives and the young couples began to stroll along the promenade in opposite directions.

"We used to come here on holiday when I was a child," Edward said. "We stayed at a boarding house a bit further along. The landlady had a boy about the same age as me and we went looking for fossils together; on the cliffs up there."

"Did you find any?"

"Oh yes. I took a bucketful back with me every year."

"You must have quite a collection."

"No. Somehow or the other Mum managed to get rid of them."

"Did you mind?"

"Not really. There was always next year."

They went to the promenade rail and looked down.

"Not much chance of going down for a paddle," Edward said, as they surveyed the rolls of barbed wire strung out along the beach midway to the sea.

"What is it for, Edward?"

"The beach has probably been mined and the barbed wire is to stop our people from getting blown up and to delay the Germans getting a foothold should there be an invasion."

Anne shivered involuntarily and Edward put an arm around her

"Come on. Put your best foot forward and I'll see if I can find the cafe where we used to go for coffee and ice cream."

The five lovely, carefree days they spent together in Brightbourne soon passed and it was time for Edward to return to his unit. Before he had gone on leave, he had arranged for Anne to stay at a small hotel in

Woodstock and had obtained a sleeping out pass, so that their honey-moon could be extended. But, eventually, he had to resume his normal duties and so once more he accompanied Anne to the station and waved goodbye to her as the train sped away to London.

CHAPTER 16

Her mother-in-law was waiting at Victoria Station to meet Anne's train. She kissed her fondly and said, "I thought it would be nice for us to have lunch together before you have to catch your train home."

"Yes, thank you. I'd like that."

Anne didn't feel hungry, but it was a kind thought and she was pleased that Ellen Lewis had come to meet her. She was feeling a little down and Ellen, sensing this, chatted brightly in an effort to cheer her up.

They found a British Restaurant not far from the station and had a passable lunch, considering that rationing was becoming more evident and the Government had set a limit on how much could be spent on restaurant meals.

"This is not a patch on your mother's cooking," Ellen said and Anne could only nod in agreement.

Ellen asked Anne if much had changed in Brightbourne since they had spent their holidays there when Edward was a child.

"Edward said that apart from the barbed wire on the beach, nothing seemed to have changed much. He showed me the house where you used to stay and where he and the boy from the boarding house went looking for shells and the cafe where you had coffee and ice cream is still there."

Ellen had laughed when Anne told her about Edward's shell collections.

"He was such a little hoarder. I'd have had a house full of shells if he had had his way."

She looked at her watch.

"What time does your train leave? I think perhaps it's time we were on our way."

Ellen paid the bill and they made their way back to the station. As they waited for the train, Anne said, "If ever you feel you would like a weekend away, come and stay with us."

"If you want to come up to town for a shopping spree, let me know," Ellen replied.

"I will. Thanks for lunch. Goodbye."

"Goodbye. Take care. Perhaps you could come and stay with us next time Edward gets leave."

CHAPTER 17

Anne arrived back in Elmersdale in time to catch the last bus going past the farm. As she walked up the lane, her suitcase getting heavier by the minute, everything looked the same as it always had. 'But I'm not the same,' she thought.

Her mother was in the kitchen preparing the evening meal and left what she was doing, to give her a hug.

"Did you have a nice time?"

"Yes. It was a lovely hotel and Edward knew Brightbourne quite well. His family used to spend their holidays there when he was little. Mrs. Lewis met me at Victoria and we had lunch together."

"That was nice for you. Would you like a cup of tea?"

"Yes please. Where's Dad?"

"He's out doing the rounds with Ben."

"Tom's brother?"

"Yes."

"Has Tom gone then?"

"Yes. He stayed on until last Friday, showing Ben around the farm, and then he had to go. Dad's finding it hard work knocking the lad into shape."

Anne finished her cup of tea. She was dog tired, but, "I'll go and give Dad a hand," she said and went into the lobby to change into her gumboots.

She found her father in the cow byre talking to a gangling youth; a younger looking version of Tom. Her father looked up as he heard her footfall.

"Hallo lass. I didn't expect to see you."

He turned to the boy and said, "You can get off home now Ben. Anne will finish the rounds with me. Mind you're here by half past six in the morning."

"Yes, Mr. Piper. Goodnight. Goodnight Miss."

"I'm glad you're back Anne. That boy hasn't the sense he was born with."

"Give him a chance, Dad," Anne laughed. "He's only been here a week."

"Aye, perhaps you're right."

They completed the nightly check on the livestock and linking arms made their way back to the farmhouse.

"Is everything all right lass? You look a bit down."

"I'm OK Dad. Just a bit tired."

"Some of your mother's home cooking and a good night's sleep and you'll be right as rain."

"Yes, I expect so," said Anne.

"I think I'll have an early night," Anne said to her parents after supper.

"Yes, you do that. It's been a long day for you," her mother said.

"Ben and I will manage in the morning. You have a bit of a lie-in."

"Thanks Dad. Goodnight."

As Anne got ready for bed, she thought back to the short time she and Edward had spent together. Tonight she would sleep alone again. She wanted to be with him, not miles away, here at the farm. She was already missing him so much, she ached.

Anne slept fitfully and was wakened by the daylight streaming through her bedroom window, where she had left the curtains drawn back last night. She felt heavy eyed and was glad her father had given her the option of a lie-in. She was not ready to face the world yet. She lay there wondering how Edward felt this morning. Did he ache for her as much as she did for him?

Sounds from outside interrupted her thoughts. The clanking of the milk churns being loaded onto the cart; the clatter of cattle hoofs on the cobbles in the farm yard and the tuneless whistle of the postman, as he cycled up to the farm door. This last sound galvanized her into action. Perhaps there would be a letter from Edward. She flung on her dressing-gown and ran down the stairs to collect the post before making her way into the kitchen.

"You look better this morning. Ready for your breakfast?"

"Yes. I was hoping there would be a letter from Edward."

"You only left him yesterday. I don't suppose he has had much time to write a letter," her mother said.

"No. I suppose not."

The time away from the farm had unsettled Anne somewhat, but she knew that, like Edward, she would have to 'resume normal duties', so after breakfast, she went back upstairs to wash and change into her working clothes and then went to find her father and Ben.

Chapter 18

When he returned to duty after the honeymoon, Edward too felt unsettled. He had misgivings about his ability to continue working in intelligence at M15 and thought he would be better employed using his journalistic skills as a war correspondent, rather than kicking his heels at Malvern. He wanted to see some action and said as much to his Commanding Officer one night in the Mess.

Some weeks later towards the end of September 1940, he was summoned to his CO's office and told that his application for a transfer had come through. He was to report to the War Office in London, where arrangements would be set in motion to expedite his new posting.

Edward wrote to Anne and said that he would be in London on official business and hoped it would be possible for her to come and spend some time with him.

"Of course you must go," her father said, when Anne had read the letter to him and her mother.

"We can manage without you for a few days."

"Yes, we'll manage," her mother agreed, but she thought to herself, 'Something's up.' Edward hadn't had any leave since the honeymoon and now he was in London on official business.

Excited at the thought of seeing Edward again, Anne hurriedly packed a suitcase.

"Give our best wishes to Mr. and Mrs. Lewis," her mother said.

"Yes, I will."

It was dark when Anne arrived at Victoria Station and she felt disorientated. She hadn't had time to let anyone know she was coming, so there was no one to meet her. She decided against taking the tube and walked out of the station in the hope of finding a taxi. Although it was quite late, there seemed to be crowds of people about; all in a hurry. There was a long queue at the taxi rank, but eventually she reached the head and getting into a cab, she gave the driver the address in Canonbury.

The streets were unlit and the taxi driver was going through areas unfamiliar to her. The cabbie slowed down and called through to her"What number Miss?"

Anne told him and the taxi crawled along until, in the dim light, she recognised the front of the Lewis' house.

"Here. Just here," she called to him.

She got out of the taxi, paid the driver off and gave him a tip. The cabbie put up his flag and drove away.

Anne went up the steps and knocked on the door. She waited for what seemed an age before she heard the swish of a curtain being drawn back and the door opened. Ellen Lewis was surprised to see her daughter-in-law standing on the doorstep.

"Anne. Come in. Is everything all right? Why didn't you let us know you were coming?"

"I didn't have time. I only got Edward's letter today. Is he here?"

"No. He won't be back until later; if at all."

Anne's heart sank.

"Leave your case in the hall, dear. We can take it upstairs later," and she led Anne down the dimly lit hallway and into the sitting room and offered her a drink.

"No thanks, but I'd love a cup of tea."

"Yes, of course."

Anne followed her into the kitchen and handed a shopping bag to Ellen.

"Mum sent you a few things."

"Oh, thank you. That was kind of her. How are things at home?" Ellen asked, as she put the half a dozen fresh eggs, a pat of butter and a small cheese wrapped in waxed paper into her larder.

"They're fine. Dad has had to plough up some of our fallow fields and we now have a couple of pigs. Ben has settled in and is a whizz with the tractor and plough and Mum still goes to WI, but she doesn't have time to be in the WVS and Lady Brewster wasn't too pleased about that. What about you?"

"It's been a bit hectic at times. We've an Anderson shelter in the garden and I'm pretty well organised when the siren goes off, but I worry about Frank working so late in the city. Have you had any air raids?"

"One or two; nothing serious. We think they may have been targeting the army camp a few miles out of Elmersdale."

"I was just going to have dinner. I minced what was left of the weekend joint and made a shepherd's pie. Shall I set the table in the dining room? I could light a fire in there."

"No. Let's save on the coal and eat in the kitchen."

They finished their dinner and Ellen made some coffee, but there was still no sign of Edward or his father returning home.

"It's getting late," Ellen said. "We may as well go to bed and try to get a few hours' sleep before the siren goes."

They went out into the hall and Anne picked up her case and followed her mother-in-law upstairs and into Edward's room.

"Have you brought any slacks and a thick jumper with you?"

"No," said Anne. "I'm afraid I packed in rather a hurry."

"Never mind. Edward's winter dressing-gown is still in his wardrobe. That will be quite warm and easy to put on over your night-clothes and there are still some of his socks in the drawer."

She took them out and laid them on a bedside chair.

"If the siren goes, I'll come and fetch you. Get dressed as quickly as you can and we'll go down into the shelter."

She kissed Anne goodnight and went along the landing to her own bedroom.

Anne lay awake for a long time, wondering where Edward was and why he had not come home. She was just dozing off when the wail of the air raid siren jolted her awake. The sound turned her stomach over. There was a knock on the bedroom door.

"Anne; come down to the kitchen, quick as you can."

Anne was out of bed in a flash. Putting on the dressing-gown, she thrust her feet into her shoes and remembering to pick up Edward's socks, she hurried down to the kitchen, where she found Ellen with a shopping basket in one hand and a small kettle in the other. Switching off the kitchen light, Ellen opened the back door. As they made their way down the path to the shelter, above them they could see the beams of the searchlights already criss-crossing the sky.

A piece of sacking covered the opening of the shelter and pushing this aside, Ellen stepped down three shallow wooden steps; then, putting down the basket and kettle, she turned to help Anne. The shelter was dark and smelt of damp and Anne shivered, whether from the cold night air, or fear, she couldn't decide; probably both.

There were two bunk-like seats either side of the shelter and at the far end, a small table. Ellen took an old piece of blanket from one of the bunks and fastened it over the inside of the opening. She switched on a torch, so that she could see to put a match to the night-light, which stood in a saucer on the table, alongside a camping stove.

"We'll soon have a warming cup of Bovril," she said.

Above them they could hear the drone of aircraft and the sound of the ack-ack gun, sited in a nearby square, firing. Both Ellen and Anne bent double and covered their heads with their hands, as they heard the scream and then the crump of bombs falling.

"That was close," said Ellen.

"I've left my gas mask in the house."

"Don't worry dear. It will still be there in the morning."

'If I live to see the morning,' thought a terrified Anne.

The Bovril was indeed comforting and the two women dozed fitfully, until the 'all clear' sounded in the early hours of the morning. Ellen collected her basket and kettle, pulled aside the blanket and the piece of sacking and climbed stiffly out of the shelter. Anne climbed out after her. The sky above them was a clear indigo blue and the morning star shone brightly, but the acrid smell of burning filled the air as they retraced their steps back into the house. In the kitchen, Ellen put the kettle on. She filled two hot water bottles and she and Anne went back upstairs to bed.

Ellen drew back her bedroom curtains before getting into bed and looked out of windowpanes buttressed by strips of brown sticky paper. On the opposite side of the road, she saw a huge gap in the middle of what had been an elegant row of semi-detached Edwardian villas. She hurried to Edward's room and knocked on the door.

"Anne dear," she called. "I don't think we should go back to bed."

Anne opened the door, still in Edward's dressing-gown and socks.

"Why? What has happened?"

"The bombs – last night. One fell on the houses opposite. I expect the warden will be coming soon. We might have to leave the house."

She looked at Anne's white face.

"Perhaps we should go down to the kitchen and make a cup of tea first."

Edward had been kept late at the War Office that night and unaware that Anne had come to London, he phoned his father's office at 'The Chronicle' to see if he was still working. He hoped to persuade his father to come home with him, rather than sleep on the couch in his office, as he sometimes did if he worked very late.

They left 'The Chronicle' building in the early hours of the morning and caught a night bus to Canonbury. At the top of the road where they lived, they were stopped by a policeman standing guard.

"What's going on Officer?" Frank Lewis said.

"A stray bomb dropped on a couple of houses last night. I'm afraid you can't go down there sir."

"I live here, Officer. I must go. I must find out if my wife is safe."

"And you sir?" the policeman said, looking at Edward.

"He's my son. On leave. You must let us through."

"I'll have a word with the warden. Just a minute sir."

He came back a few minutes later and asked them on which side of the road they lived.

"That's opposite the bombed houses. Just be very careful where you tread sir," and he allowed them through.

Edward and his father stepped over the barrier and hurried along, aghast at the devastation and fearful of what they might find when they arrived at their house. Hastily Frank inserted his key in the lock and opened his front door. He ran through the house calling his wife's name. She appeared at the kitchen door, still in her night-clothes, and behind his mother Edward saw Anne in his dressing-gown. Frank Lewis held his wife close.

"Thank God you're safe," he said.

Edward gathered Anne into his arms and said, "What are you doing here?"

"You wrote and asked me to come," she said, close to tears.

"Why didn't you let someone know you were coming?"

"I didn't have time and you didn't say how long you were going to be in London."

"No. I'm sorry. I'm just glad that you are safe." He turned to his mother and said, "Are you all right Mum?"

Frank Lewis hugged his daughter-in-law and kissed her forehead.

"Thank God you are both safe," he said again.

"I've just made a pot of tea. I think we could all do with a cup."

Sitting at the kitchen table drinking their tea, Anne was still visibly shaken, but Ellen kept a tight rein on herself.

There was a knock on the front door and Frank went to open it. An air-raid warden stood there.

"Just checking on the occupants of the houses sir."

"All present and correct here," said Frank. "Is it safe for us to stay in the house?"

"For the time being, sir. The blast from the bomb seems to have gone away from this side of the road."

"What about the Hopkins' and the Rouses?"

"They were in the Anderson. Shaken up a bit, as you can imagine, but safe. The neighbours climbed over the garden walls after the 'all-clear' went and dug away until they could get them out. They have been taken to the church hall in Britannia Row. They're not the only ones there. It's been quite a heavy night."

"Thank you for calling. Let us know if there is anything we can do."

"That's all right, sir. All in the line of duty." He touched the brim of his tin hat and went to knock on the door of the next house.

Frank came back with the information the warden had given him and suggested that they all try to get a few hours' sleep.

As Edward and Anne lay cuddled together in his single bed, he deliberated over the best way to tell his young wife what his next posting entailed. Now, clearly, was not the time.

"I'll see if I can get a weekend pass and come down to Elmersdale," he said. "And you must go home today. I can't think why I ever thought of asking you to come to London."

"I've missed you, Edward."

"And I've missed you, sweetheart, but you are safer at the farm."

They had both been frightened by what might have happened and found comfort in their lovemaking, before falling asleep in each other's arms.

Chapter 19

Ellen went with Anne to Victoria Station and as the number thirty-eight bus took a diverted route, they could see just how much damage the air-raid had caused. Anne said again to her mother-in-law, “Come and stay with us if the bombing gets too bad.”

“We’ll have to see. I can’t come without Frank and with Edward being in London for the time being, it’s not really feasible.”

She saw Anne to her train and they kissed each other goodbye.

“Take care of yourself, my dear. Give my regards to your mother and father.”

“I will. You take care of yourself too. Goodbye.”

The train journey home seemed interminable to Anne. She tried to doze, but memories of the night she had spent in the garden shelter with Ellen kept flashing through her mind and she was glad when the train finally pulled into Elmersdale Station. She handed in her ticket and walked out of the station and towards the bus stop. She looked at the timetable and realised that she had just missed a bus and would have to wait half an hour before the next one came along. The cafe in the High Street was closed and so a despondent Anne had no option but to wait in the cold.

John Perry was just coming out of the ‘Black Bull’ and was on his way home when he saw Anne waiting at the bus stop and went over to speak to her.

"Hallo Anne. How are you? You've just missed the bus."

"Yes, I know. I've been up to London to see Edward."

"How is he? And Frank and Ellen?"

"They're OK. Edward was on some kind of official business and Mr. Lewis is working all hours and I was caught up in an air-raid and spent half the night in their shelter in the garden with Mrs. Lewis. It was very frightening and the bomb damage in London is dreadful." The words came tumbling out.

"My car is parked just over the road. I'll give you a lift home."

Anne said very little on the journey and John Perry let her be.

He dropped her off at the bottom of the farm lane. Anne thanked him for the lift and they said goodnight. John Perry wondered just how frightening her experience had been. By the look of her, the air-raid had affected her badly.

Her father was coming out of the barn and seeing Anne, he came towards her and took her case from her.

"Whatever's the matter lass?" he said as she burst into tears. "Let's get you inside and you can tell us all about it."

Nancy Piper took one look at her daughter's tear-stained face and came and put her arms around her.

"There, there, my little lass. Come and sit down and tell us what has happened. A drop of brandy, I think, Sam."

Sam Piper nodded and went to fetch glasses and the brandy and brought them to the table.

"Is it Edward?" her mother asked her.

"No."

"Mr. and Mrs. Lewis?"

"No."

Sam and Nancy looked at one another, relieved at this news.

They waited while Anne recovered herself and took a sip of brandy. Gradually she was able to tell them about the air-raid and how frightened she had been.

"There was a horrible screaming noise and then, when the bomb had dropped, everything shook and I thought the shelter would collapse on top of us. When we came out of the shelter after the 'all-clear' went, there was a dreadful smell of burning and there was dust everywhere. We went back into the house and I was just getting into bed when Mrs. Lewis came and knocked on the door. She said that a bomb had dropped on the houses opposite. Her neighbours' houses weren't there anymore. There was just a pile of rubble."

"Were the people in the houses hurt?" her father asked.

"No, Dad. They were in a shelter in their garden, like we were. The people in the houses next to them clambered over their garden walls and dug until they managed to free their neighbours."

"Where was Mr. Lewis?"

"He was working late in the City and so was Edward. They didn't come home until after the air-raid was over. Mr. Lewis was as white as a sheet when he came into the house and Edward said he didn't want me to stay in London any longer."

"Did you ask Mrs. Lewis to come and stay with us?"

"Yes, I did Mum. She said she would think about it, but with Mr. Lewis running his paper and Edward in London, she didn't see how she could for the time being."

"Well, at least everyone is safe and you are home. That's the main thing," said her father.

"Yes, I suppose so. Edward said he would see if he could get a weekend pass and come to see us."

"Well, there you are then." Nancy Piper was at a loss to know how best to comfort her daughter.

That night, as they lay in bed, Nancy and Sam went back over what Anne had told them.

"There is no doubt it has certainly shaken her up," Sam said.

"Whatever was Edward thinking of asking her to go up to London?"

"Well, fair play, he just wanted to see her and he didn't know she would go haring off as soon as she got his letter. He couldn't have known there was going to be an air-raid that night. There has been a lull in the bombing lately."

"What do you think Edward is doing, working in London all of a sudden, Sam?"

"Well, if he gets this weekend pass, I expect we'll find out," Sam said.

Chapter 20

Edward knew that before he left 'Piper's Farm' that weekend, he would have to tell Anne that he was being posted overseas and that this would be the last time they would see each other for a while. He was due to embark on a troopship sailing out of Glasgow sometime during the first week in November. He had told his father, as much as he was allowed to, about what he would be doing, but had asked him not to tell his mother until he was on his way to North Africa. The matter of telling his wife, he knew, was up to him.

Nancy Piper sensed Edward's unease as soon as he arrived at the farm on a Friday evening towards the end of October 1940. He wasn't his usual, cheerful self and when he accompanied Sam to make the evening check on the livestock, she knew something was brewing.

Anne was happy that Edward had managed to get a weekend pass, but she too noticed that there was something troubling him. She waited until they had gone to bed before she said, "Is there something you want to tell me, Edward?"

"It can wait," he prevaricated. "Do you still love your poor soldier?"

"You know I do."

"Show me then," he said and took her in his arms.

The next morning her father said, "Ben and I can manage today, lass. You and Edward haven't really had much time together lately."

And her mother added. "I've made up a picnic for you."

Anne thought, 'What is going on?'

Edward said, "Let's take the bikes and see where we land up."

"Yes, all right."

Anne put the food her mother had prepared for them into a rucksack and put it in the basket on the front of her bike; then she and Edward cycled down the lane and away from the farm.

It was a beautiful October morning; the sun was just beginning to dispel the morning mist. The leaves on the trees were taking on their autumn colour and there were still some blackberries on the roadside bramble bushes.

"I don't think I ever really appreciated autumn until I came to live in Elmersdale," Edward remarked.

Anne smiled at her husband waxing lyrical.

They had been cycling alongside Colonel Brewster's estate and had come to a point where the estate ended and fields led down to the River Elmer. Anne dismounted and confronted Edward.

"Stop beating about the bush and tell me what this is all about."

Edward got off his bike and propped it beside Anne's, against the estate wall.

"Let's go down to the river," he said and taking the rucksack out of the basket, he set off at a brisk pace.

Anne followed him until they came to the river bank, and slightly breathless, she sat down on a fallen log.

"Well?" she said.

"Let's have elevenses first. Has your mother put some scones in that bag?"

"Edward Lewis; will you get on with it?"

"I'm being posted overseas," he blurted out. "I'm sailing next week."

"Is that why you've been in London?"

"Yes. I'm part of a film unit. I've been on a course and now that we have completed it, our crew is ready for action."

"I see. So it's just this weekend then?"

"Yes."

Anne sat quietly, taking in what Edward had told her; then she sighed.

"Well, that's the war for you," and passed him a cup of tea from the thermos flask and a buttered scone.

Chapter 21

As usual Anne and her parents went into the parlour to listen to the nine o'clock news on the Home Service. She felt a wave of nausea overwhelm her as Alvar Lidell announced that London had suffered a series of severe air-raids, with the loss of many lives. The City had been particularly targeted and eight Wren churches had been bombed. She had been sick quite a few times lately and put it down to being worried about her in-laws being in the thick of the bombing and to the fact that she hadn't heard from Edward since he wrote to her from Glasgow before he set sail.

One morning, when she couldn't face breakfast yet again, Nancy Piper looked at her daughter's wan face.

"How long have you been feeling like this?"

"I don't know. A few weeks, I suppose."

"Have you had your monthlies?!"

Anne thought for a moment. "Well, I'm a bit overdue."

"Are you? How much overdue?"

"My last one was a few weeks before I went up to London."

"You had a nasty shock when you were there. It might be that."

But remembering how ardently she and Edward had made love the weekend before he went away, Anne thought otherwise.

Chapter 22

Christmas was drawing close, but few people had the heart to celebrate. The shops closed early, as the blackout stopped people from staying in Elmersdale town centre longer than they needed to. The street lamps were unlit and blackout curtains withheld any light from the houses. No candles were placed in windows to welcome the Christ Child. No groups of carol singers went from house to house singing 'Tis the season to be jolly'.

Nancy Piper was doing her best, in the light of the restrictions imposed by rationing, to prepare for the season of goodwill. She was hard put to find the ingredients for a decent Christmas Pudding, having used quite a lot from her store cupboard for the wedding cake.

Colonel Brewster had held a shoot early in December and Sam had come back with a brace of pheasants, which now hung out in the lobby by the back door.

The 'Gazette' had published a series of recipes on 'Making the Most of Your Rations' and Nancy had made a presentable boiled fruit cake from one of them. The 'marzipan' was made from soya flour, as ground almonds were unavailable.

"Perhaps it won't be so bad after all," she said to Anne, as she handed down the box of Christmas decorations from the loft.

Christmas Eve dawned bright and frosty. Nancy spent much of the day in her kitchen, busy putting the finishing touches to her preparations for Christmas Day. Her sister and her husband Arthur, and Eileen were coming to spend the day at the farm and she was glad that there would be a bit of company. Sam was becoming increasingly worried about the number of new regulations from the Ministry and Anne was fretting about Edward and his parents.

'Everyone could do with cheering up,' she thought.

Nancy and Sam Piper went to the midnight service on Christmas Eve, but Anne felt too tired and said she would go to the Christmas Morning Service and went to bed early.

She stood by the lych gate in the cold frosty air, talking to her aunt and cousin after the service, while her uncle went to fetch his car to take them back to the farm.

"I always enjoy the Reverend Williams' sermon on Christmas Day," said her aunt. "Every year he brings something new to the story, doesn't he?"

"Yes," replied Anne, "but wasn't it cold in the church?"

"I hope your Dad has a drop of something warming lined up," her uncle said, as he opened the car door for them.

Eileen slipped her arm in Anne's as they sat in the back of the car.

"Have you heard from Edward lately, Anne?"

"In a roundabout way. He left a letter and a package with his mother before he went away and she posted it to me a few days ago with a Christmas card from her and Mr. Lewis and a pair of silk stockings."

"That was nice of her. What did Edward send you?"

"It was a pearl necklace," and she opened the top of her coat a fraction to show Eileen.

Anne opened the farmhouse door and they all went into the parlour, where her father was waiting with a glass of 'something warming' for her uncle. Her mother came from the kitchen carrying a tray with cups of tea for the women.

The pheasants were done to a turn; the pudding surprisingly good and Aunt Elsie had brought a bottle of her elderberry wine to add to the festivities.

"You've done us proud today, Nancy," Arthur said.

"Yes, it was a lovely dinner," Elsie agreed.

They sat at the dining table reminiscing about Christmases past, until Sam said, "Time to listen to the King's Christmas Broadcast."

He and Arthur went into the parlour and after Sam had turned on the wireless, they settled themselves in armchairs either side of the fireplace. Nancy and her sister raised their eyebrows and began to clear the table.

"You go and sit down too, Mum, and you Aunt Elsie. Eileen and I will wash the dishes, won't we?"

"Yes, you both go and put your feet up."

The two sisters went to join their husbands and after listening to the King's speech, they settled themselves on the comfortable old sofa. Presently all four were snoozing.

"I could do with a breath of fresh air," Anne said, as she put the last of the dishes away. "How about you?"

"We'd better wrap up warm. The frost hasn't melted all day."

The girls walked briskly down the lane, chatting about the presents they had been given. Eileen turned to Anne.

"You look a bit peaky. Is everything all right?"

"Yes," said Anne, not willing to share her secret with her cousin until she had heard from Edward that he had received her letter telling him about the baby "With only Ben to help us, it's been hard work to get all the jobs done."

The girls came back into the warmth of the kitchen, their cheeks glowing from the cold. Anne put the kettle on, took the cake from the tin and put mince pies to warm in the Aga. Eileen set a tray with cups and saucers. They took the tea things into the parlour, just as their parents were rousing from their naps. Anne's father stretched and yawned. Her mother and her aunt sat up and smoothed down their dresses. Uncle

Arthur, seeing the tea tray said, "Ah, a cup of tea. Just what the doctor ordered."

When Anne had finished her tea, her father said to her, "Play us a few carols Anne."

She sat down at the piano and began to play. After a while, she turned to her uncle and said, "Come and sing for us uncle."

Arthur had a light baritone voice and was an asset in the church choir. He also had a wicked sense of humour. Anne began to play 'Come into the garden Maud', knowing full well that her uncle would sing his own version and he soon had them all laughing at his parody.

"Your turn, Sam. What about 'Sam, Sam pick up tha' musket'?"

Sam shook his head, but with everyone urging him on, he began to recite the monologue made famous by the actor Stanley Holloway.

Dusk was beginning to fall before Elsie, Arthur and Eileen left the farm. There were fond farewells all round.

"We'll expect you for supper tomorrow, Nancy," said her sister.

"Do you want me to bring anything?"

"Some of that ham wouldn't go amiss."

"Arthur, really," said his wife. "But I wouldn't say no though. It was very tasty."

Eileen whispered to Anne, "Tom's home on leave and Mum said I can invite him to supper tomorrow."

"Still going strong then?"

Eileen nodded.

"I'll come with you to the end of the lane, Arthur, and open the gate for you."

Before Sam got out of the car to open the gate, Arthur said, "I don't know how much longer I'll be able to run the car, Sam. There's talk of rationing petrol for non-essential purposes."

Arthur and Elsie ran the newsagents in the High Street and besides using his car for pleasure, he also used it to collect the London papers from the station in the morning and evening.

"I don't know if bringing the news to people would be classed as essential. I hear say that Lady Brewster is thinking of using a pony and trap."

The two men chuckled at the thought of the buxom Lady Brewster kitted out in her WVS uniform trotting about the countryside.

"Perhaps she'll hire it out to you, Arthur."

"Rather that than trying to balance the bundles on that old penny farthing she still keeps in the stables. Goodnight Sam. I'll see you tomorrow."

Sam walked back to the farm still chuckling. He and Arthur had known each other since boyhood and had served together in the Brewster Estate Battalion during the First World War. Even in the darkest days Arthur had remained cheerful and kept everyone's spirits up.

'He was a card was Arthur', Sam thought.

Chapter 23

By the end of 1940, Britain was effectively under siege and it seemed that the country might be starved into submission. Sam Piper, along with other farmers, had been given a directive from the Ministry of Agriculture and Fisheries to plough acres of grassland and wasteland, so that they could become more productive. It was true that all of the farmers in the Elmersdale district had formed a kind of co-operative to help each other out, but it seemed that everyone was becoming overburdened. Sam had had to invest in a tractor and ploughing paraphernalia and being unused to mechanics, had left it to Ben, who took to it like a duck to water.

The winter was harsh that year and the postman struggled valiantly up to the farm, knee deep in snow, to deliver the mail. Letters from Edward came sporadically and although Anne wrote to him regularly, she knew from the questions they asked each other and the answers received, that some of their letters had gone astray.

Robert Francis Lewis was born in Elmersdale Cottage Hospital on the 28th of July 1941 and Anne wrote to Edward and sent him a photograph of his son. Edward, somewhere in the Western Desert, following the progress of the Eighth Army, didn't receive her letter until weeks later. He wrote back immediately, saying how proud he was of her and that he was delighted with their son.

Sam Piper was finding it hard going with just him and Ben working all the daylight hours and more on the farm. Anne helped out when she could, but a lot of her time was taken up with young Robert and even with Nancy doing more than her fair share, some things were still being left undone. Sam had no option but to apply to the District Commissioner to send him help in the shape of two girls from the Women's Land Army.

Late on a bitterly cold afternoon in January 1942, Anne went to meet the two girls at Elmersdale Station. They were instantly recognisable in their very new uniforms. They also looked very young. Anne put on a bright smile and went towards them.

"Hallo," she said. "I'm Anne Lewis from 'Piper's Farm'."

The two girls introduced themselves.

"I'm Jessie Silverton. Pleased to meet you," and she held out a small well manicured hand.

"And I'm Elizabeth – Lizzie – Lewis. How do you do?"

Anne, who had recently passed her driving test, said, "I've parked the truck out in the station yard."

The girls followed Anne out of the station, put their cases in the back of the truck and climbed in beside Anne in the cab. On the way back to the farm, Anne asked the girls how they had come to be in the WLA.

"For a healthy, happy job – join the Women's Land Army," they chorused.

"I liked the uniform better than the ATS or the WAAF," said Jessie.

"I really wanted to join the WRNS," said Lizzie, "but I'm not a very good sailor. I went to the Isle of Wight on holiday once and I was ill all the way over on the ferry."

"What did you do before you joined up?"

"I worked in the accounts department of the Army and Navy Store in the Strand," said Jessie.

"I worked as a shorthand typist in a solicitor's office in Lincoln's Inn," Lizzie said.

Neither of these two places rang a bell with Anne. They sounded like Londoners. She would ask her mother-in-law the next time she wrote to her to tell her how little Robert was progressing.

"So how did you meet?"

"At the training camp," said Jessie. "I was fed up with working in an office. My Mum thought it would be too dangerous in the forces, so as soon as I turned eighteen, I went and joined the WLA."

"What about you Lizzie?"

"I didn't want to go into any of the other women's services or work in munitions. I thought it might be nice to work with animals."

"Did you get much training?"

"Four weeks," both girls said together.

'Only four weeks,' thought Anne. 'Dad will have a fit.'

"We are almost here. Will one of you get out and open the gate?"

Lizzie got out and waited while Anne drove the truck into the lane leading to the farm, being careful to secure the gate before she climbed back into the cab.

Nancy Piper heard the truck coming up the lane and went to open the door to welcome the girls. She took one look at them in their ill fitting uniforms. One couldn't have been much more than five feet tall and looked as if she could do with a good meal inside her. The other was a tall willowy girl, who looked as if a gust of wind would blow her over.

'They're babies,' she thought. 'Sam will have a fit.'

She said, "Come in girls. Leave your bags in the hall. I expect you could do with a cup of tea."

The girls took off their hats and greatcoats and followed Anne and her mother into the stone flagged kitchen, their eyes widening as they took in the table set for the evening meal.

"Mr. Piper will be in presently. He and Ben, that's our farmhand, are just finishing work for the day. Sit yourselves down and drink your tea while we wait for them."

Sam Piper and Ben came across the farm yard.

"Looks like Anne's back Mr. Piper," said Ben.

"Yes. Let's go and see what the wind's blown in."

He came into the kitchen, followed by Ben.

"Evening," Sam said.

Jessie and Lizzie stood up and returned his greeting.

'Cripes,' thought Ben, looking at the two city waifs. 'Mr. Piper will have his work cut out with these two.' He grinned at the girls. "Evening," he said.

Anne introduced Lizzie and Jessie to her father.

"Will you stop and have a bite to eat with us Ben?"

"Thanks Mrs. Piper," and he went to join Mr. Piper, who was washing his hands at the kitchen sink.

When they were all seated at the table eating their supper, Sam Piper addressed the girls.

"What sort of things did they teach you at the training centre?"

"Everything," said Jessie.

"How long did you say your training was?" said Sam.

"Four weeks," Lizzie answered. "Just the basics really, but we're willing to learn."

"And we'll work hard," said Jessie, eager to please.

Just how hard they would have to work, they had no idea.

Anne and her mother began to clear away the supper dishes. Lizzie and Jessie asked if they could help with the washing up, but Mrs. Piper said "No" to their offer. She looked across at Sam...

"Perhaps now would be a good time to talk to the girls about the way you run the farm."

"It's almost time for the news," said Sam. "I think they should get a good night's rest. We'll talk about it in the morning."

And with that, he picked up the paper from the dresser and went into the front parlour, saying "goodnight" to Ben as he passed.

'Four weeks! I hope I've done the right thing,' he thought.

"I'll be off home then. Thanks for supper Mrs. Piper. See you in the morning. Six o'clock sharp," Ben said wickedly, looking at the city girls' open mouths.

"You go in and listen to the news, Mum. I'll take the girls up to their room and show them the way to the bathroom."

Lizzie and Jessie followed Anne up the steep staircase and along a narrow passage to the far end of the farmhouse. Coming from the warmth of the kitchen, the upper part of the farmhouse was cold and draughty.

Anne opened a door and said, "This will be your room. The bathroom is at the end of the passage. I'll come and knock on your door when it's free in the morning. Once you get used to our routine, you'll be fine. Goodnight. Sleep well."

"This looks quite comfortable doesn't it Lizzie? Which bed do you want?"

"I don't mind. This one by the window will suit me."

The girls sat on the beds covered with white jacquard counterpanes and separated by a bow fronted mahogany chest of drawers. Jessie went over to a big pine wardrobe and opened the double doors.

"Blimey," she exclaimed. "You could get Buckingham Palace in here."

Tired though the girls were, neither slept well. It was so quiet. They missed the noise of traffic and they were waiting for the sound of the air-raid warning, which never came.

Anne knocked on their door at a quarter to six the next morning. She came into the room and drew back the curtains. Frost patterns glistened on the inside of the windowpanes. It was still dark as she gently shook the girls awake.

"The bathroom is all yours," she said to the two sleepy girls.

"Come down to the kitchen as soon as you're dressed. We usually have a cup of tea before we go to the milking parlour, then we come back for breakfast about eight o'clock."

Chapter 24

After a quick visit to the bathroom, the still drowsy girls made their way down to the farm kitchen on the first day as working land girls.

Much to Sam's surprise, Lizzie and Jessie settled in well. Their four weeks' training had only touched on the many jobs that needed doing on the farm, but they proved to be willing and quick to learn and tackled some of the most back-breaking tasks cheerfully; added to which the skills they brought from their former working lives proved invaluable to Sam in solving his paperwork problem.

"Just as well to keep our hand in," said Jessie, as she surveyed the calluses on her now less than well manicured hands. Most evenings Lizzie and Jessie joined Anne and her parents in the front room after the evening meal, to listen to the wireless or play cards. Other times they tackled Sam's paperwork at the kitchen table. With his labour problem solved, Sam became less harassed; Nancy had more time to indulge her little grandson and Anne, kept busy working alongside the two land girls, had less time to worry about Edward.

Occasionally Anne went with the girls when they cycled into Elmersdale to go to the pictures. They knew that Anne's husband was somewhere in the Middle East and when the newsreel showed pictures of the battle zones, she would watch closely in the hope of getting a glimpse of him or his film unit. Cycling back to the farm after one such outing, Jessie said, "What are they going to do with all those prisoners of war?"

"When Dad came back from market this week, he heard that there are rumours that the army camp on Colonel Brewster's land is going to be moved elsewhere and that it is going to become a prisoner of war camp."

"But we saw thousands of them on the newsreel tonight. The lines of captured soldiers seemed to stretch for miles," said Lizzie.

"You silly chump," said Jessie. "They won't all fit in that camp outside Elmersdale. I'd like to be a fly on the wall of Colonel Brewster's study when he hears about it."

"I'd like to be a fly on the wall of old Harry Oakwood's kitchen," said Anne.

All three girls knew of Mr. Oakwood's sentiments about the army camp on part of his land and were still laughing when they went into the farmhouse by way of the back door.

Nancy Piper was putting the milk saucepan on the Aga in readiness for the cups of bedtime cocoa when the girls came in.

"What's the joke?" she asked and when they told her, she said, "There's many a true word spoken in jest. I popped in to have a cup of tea with Aunt Elsie after WI this afternoon and Uncle Arthur said that the rumour is more than likely true. He was talking to John Perry in the 'Black Bull' this lunchtime and he said there's a lot of coming and going up at the camp."

A week or so later a convoy of lorries filled with soldiers passed through Elmersdale on their way to who knows where. The next day a smaller convoy arrived at the camp to make it ready to receive Italian prisoners of war. For the rest of that year, very little was known about what went on at the camp. Curious passers-by reported that there was now a high fence all around the perimeter, with sentry boxes at intervals, manned by soldiers with Bren guns.

The small town of Elmersdale was uneasy with its new inhabitants, but as time passed and nothing untoward happened, an acceptance of the situation was inevitable.

As more of the farming fraternity was called up for active service, Colonel Brewster invited the commandant of the POW camp to dinner at the Manor and broached the subject of the prisoners 'earning their keep' by helping out local farmers. He had heard that schemes of a similar nature were working in other parts of the country. The young officer said he would approach the senior Italian officer in the camp to see if under the rules of the Geneva Convention, it would be possible. After speaking to the senior officer, he arranged a meeting between him, Colonel Brewster and himself. The outcome of the meeting was that those prisoners who were willing, would be taken and collected in army trucks, supervised by British soldiers, to those farmers who were disposed to have them.

Harvest time was approaching and Sam Piper, being made aware of the work scheme by an article in the 'Gazette', went to see Colonel Brewster and was allocated six Italian POWs. Paolo Cardi was one of those sent to 'Piper's Farm' under the supervision of Sergeant Jack Cummings.

After an initial wariness, the Italians came to be accepted. They were a good-natured bunch and were appreciative of Mrs. Piper's food baskets that Lizzie and Jessie took to them while they were working in the fields. Sometimes they sang Italian folk songs as they worked and laughed and joked amongst themselves when the girls were nearby.

"I wish I could understand what they're saying," said Jessie.

"Perhaps it's just as well we don't," Lizzie replied.

But she sometimes returned the smile that the tall, darkly handsome young man they called Paolo gave her.

Jessie's sharp eyes noticed this and one evening as they were driving the cows home for milking and passed the Italian POWs waiting for the truck to take them back to camp, she said to Lizzie, "Do you fancy him?"

"Who?"

"That Paolo. He's a bit of a looker and he's always ready to give you a hand."

"You get some daft ideas, Jessie, really you do."

"No, but do you?"

"Jessie! He's the enemy. Just you remember that. Anne's husband is fighting the likes of him out in the desert."

"Sergeant Cummings says that most of them are ordinary blokes and didn't want to fight a war anyway and that's why they gave themselves up so easily."

"And he would know, of course, wouldn't he, I suppose?"

"He says a lot of them are trying to learn English and are thinking of staying here after the war is over, especially if they have no family or homes to go back to."

"Well, Paolo is not one of them. His father runs a trattoria, that's a cafe, by the seaside at Rimini and he can't wait to go home."

"Has he told you that?"

"Yes. I help him with his English and he likes to talk about his home and his family."

Lizzie didn't want to pursue this conversation any further. Jessie was nearer to the truth than she cared to think about. She did like Paolo, but the war wasn't over yet and Lizzie was far too patriotic to fraternize too closely with the enemy, helpful or not.

"If we don't get a move on and get these cows to the milking shed, we're not going to get to the pictures tonight," she told Jessie.

Paolo didn't see Lizzie as his enemy. He saw a pretty girl, who was kind and listened to him talk about his hopes and dreams once he could return home. He told her he thought that learning English would be a help to him and his father, when tourists were able to come to Rimini again. He said he thought that the soldiers who had fought in Italy would see what a beautiful country it was and would want to take their families on holiday there. Lizzie listened to him, but thought that it would be a long time before his dreams could be realised.

The Italian POWs continued to come to 'Piper's Farm' and in spite of herself, Lizzie began to think of Paolo as less of an enemy and more of a dreamy young man with whom she was falling in love and when Paolo began to include her in his dreams, she knew that he loved her too.

And then the Allies invaded mainland Italy; Mussolini fled and Italy surrendered. Negotiations took place and it was decided that as Italy had now made peace with the Allies, some Italian prisoners of war could be repatriated. Paolo was excited at this prospect and said to Lizzie, "I write to you. Send you money. You come to Rimini. We be happy Lizzie."

When Sam Piper heard that his prisoners would be going home, he decided to give them a good send off. Shortly before they were due to be repatriated, he gave a farewell party and invited family and friends to come and say goodbye to the men they had come to know and like.

Paolo and Lizzie slipped away unnoticed and went to the barn to say their goodbyes privately. As they kissed and held each other close, not knowing when they would see one another again, a fever of desperation swept through them and to assuage it, they sank to the floor of the hay byre and made love.

Their passion spent, they lay in each other's arms for a while, then Paolo kissed Lizzie tenderly and helped her to her feet.

She stood and watched as he took off his St. Christopher medallion and slipped it over her head.

"You love me Lizzie? You be my wife?"

Lizzie touched the medallion. "Yes, Paolo, I love you and I will be your wife."

Part Two

Chapter 25

When Robert retired, he and his wife Jenny had settled in Highgate Village; far enough out of central London, but close enough to Whitehall for him to keep in touch with his cronies. And it was there, late one Friday afternoon in April 1999, that Joan arrived to spend the weekend with her brother and sister-in-law. Susie came straight from work to her parents' home and Philip, knowing that his aunt was visiting, rearranged his plans and so the family spent a pleasant evening together catching up on family gossip. Neither Joan nor Robert broached the subject of the envelope found in their mother's bureau.

After breakfast on Saturday morning, Joan followed Robert into his study. She handed him the envelope and watched his face as he took it. 'He does know something about all this,' she thought. 'He's not surprised. How did he find out and why didn't he tell me?'

Jenny knocked softly on the study door before she opened it and peered in.

"Would you like some more coffee?"

"Not for the moment Jen. I think Joan and I need a little time to talk."

Jenny closed the door quietly.

"Have you seen the envelope before Robert?"

"No."

"But you knew about it. Knew about Cousin Lizzie and me?"

"Yes."

"How did you know? Who told you? How long have you known? Why didn't anyone tell me?" She could hear her voice rising.

"Calm down, Joanie dear. We thought it was for the best. Really we did."

"Who did? Who thought it was for the best?"

"Mother."

"Mother!"

"Yes, Mother and Dad, of course. It's a long story Joan."

"I'm listening."

"When mother died, she wanted her ashes to be buried beside her mother and father in St. Philip's churchyard. After the memorial service, if you remember, we all went back to 'Piper's Farm' and stayed overnight. Eileen's husband, Tom, was Grandad Piper's farmhand pre-war. After the war, he went back to work for Grandad and as he and Gran were getting on in years, Tom and his brother, Ben, took on more and more of managing the farm. When Grandad died, Tom took over the tenancy of the farm and Granny Piper went to live in Elmersdale with Great Aunt Elsie and Uncle Arthur. Eileen knew about you and Lizzie, so she wrote to Dad and said it might be a nice gesture to invite Lizzie to the memorial service. So he did. After everyone had gone to bed that night, Dad and I sat in the front parlour of the farm and he began reminiscing about how he and Mum had met. He asked me if I saw any resemblance between you and Lizzie and I couldn't honestly say that I could. Then he told me that Lizzie wasn't, in fact, his cousin, but that she had been a land girl working on Grandad Piper's farm during the war."

"But the name – Lewis," said Joan.

"Just a coincidence. Lewis is a common enough name. A happy coincidence as it turned out. There was another land girl, but Dad couldn't remember her name. At that time Dad was a war correspondent out in the desert with the Eighth Army, so Mum was still living on the farm. I was born in 1941 and Lizzie and this other girl must have come to the farm sometime in 1942."

"Who was the young man in the photo?"

"He was an Italian prisoner of war." Robert looked at the photo again. "That isn't really a uniform he is wearing. It was the overalls that the POWs had to wear. If you look closer, you can just about make out the identification tabs. I think Grandad Piper had some of them to work at harvest time and at other odd times. Mum wrote to Dad and told him that the army camp outside of Elmersdale had been turned into a POW camp. The chap in the photo was one of the prisoners who came to work on the farm. When Italy surrendered in the September of 1943, some of the Italian POWs were repatriated early and Paolo Cardi was one of them. He and Lizzie must have got together somehow, because she came to Mum in tears one day. Paolo was gone and Lizzie was pregnant. And Mum came to the rescue."

"Did Mum and Dad adopt me?"

"No. Lizzie couldn't bring herself to give you up entirely. She must have thought that perhaps one day…" He shrugged. "Who knows? Mum always kept in touch with Lizzie and if you remember she made sure that you always sent her a card on her birthday and at Christmas time."

Yes. Joan did remember her mother's insistence and now she knew why.

"So what happened?" Did Lizzie stay on at the farm?"

"Yes she did, for a while. Her mother and father had been killed in 1944, when the Germans launched the VI flying bombs on London, so she had no home to go to."

"How long did she stay on?"

"It must have been a year perhaps. Then Lizzie applied for a one year teacher training course under some government scheme after the war and Mum told her to go for it and that she would look after you for her."

"So what then, Robert?"

"The war had ended. Dad got demobbed and joined Grandfather Lewis and became a journalist on 'The Chronicle' He and Mum settled in London and everyone, except those in the know, thought you were their new baby."

"What did Dad think about all this?"

"Well, you know the old man. Do anything to keep Mum happy."

"And when Dad died and we had to sell the house, did you not mind the estate being divided equally between us?"

"No," said Robert. "To all intents and purposes, he looked upon you as his daughter and after all, you were the one who stayed at home to look after him when Mum died. And Jen and I were grateful to you for taking care of Philip and Susie while we were abroad."

'Yes,' thought Joan, remembering all the part-time jobs she had taken, when she had found it becoming increasingly difficult to care for her ailing father and cope with her demanding job as head of business studies at the local further education college.

And then, during the last year of his life, no job at all and no social life either.

"As I say," said Robert, bringing her thoughts back to the present, "Mum and Dad thought it was the best thing in the long run for you not to know about your connection with Cousin Lizzie and because she had given up hope of being with Paolo and decided to get on with her life, probably best for her too."

"I think I could do with some coffee now, Robert," Joan said. Personally, Robert thought he could do with something a little stronger.

"Right you are," he said and followed her out of his study and into the kitchen, where Jenny waited apprehensively.

After lunch on that traumatic Saturday, Susie suggested a walk on the Heath. She wanted to test out her idea of getting in touch with the other land girl, via the 'Daily Mail' column 'Missing and Found'. Joan wasn't sure. She was inclined to let sleeping dogs lie. She was shaken by the morning's revelations, but she had had a contented childhood and had been relatively happy living in ignorance of her true parentage. Might she be opening a 'Pandora's Box'? Susie, however, had the bit between her teeth. She was intrigued and wanted to find out more.

Meanwhile, Robert and Jenny discussed whether or not to give the bundle of letters that their father had found in a locked drawer in his wife's dressing-table after she had died, to Joan. They decided to wait until Susie and his sister came back from their walk, the better to judge how the land lay.

Philip was sitting out in the conservatory reading the papers when his sister and their aunt returned from their walk. On the pretence of taking him a cup of tea, Susie told him what she had suggested to their aunt.

"Susie," he said, giving her a warning look.

"Don't you want to find out more about Cousin Lizzie and her POW lover?"

"It's not really up to any of us," Philip said. "I think we should give Aunt Joan a little more time to think it over."

"Oh Philip, really; you are so stuffy," Susie said and went to find her mother and sound her out.

Sunday morning saw Robert and Joan once more in Robert's study. After much thought, he had decided that Joan should know about the letters. This time Jenny brought them all some coffee and stayed as they read through the letters, trying between them to piece together the story of the ill-fated, war time romance and its outcome.

They gathered that Paolo had returned to Rimini, where his father had a small trattoria on the sea front. Paolo had written in his broken English, how difficult life was in the aftermath of the war; of the shortages and privations his community had suffered. He enclosed his address and hoped that Lizzie would write back to him. In another letter he wrote to say that things were better. Life was beginning to reach some kind of normality. Local people still came to the trattoria and he hoped that with government compensation, he and his father might be able to expand their business. It was still a beautiful place to live and he was sure that now the war was over, tourists would come again to Rimini. 'You will be so happy here Lizzie,' he wrote.

Paolo wrote again. He had not received a reply to his letters. He wrote his address in capital letters, so that when she wrote, she would not make mistakes, as she must have done, or surely her letters would have reached him. Paolo's letters came at irregular intervals; sometimes months between them. Still he had received no letters from her. He wrote that he loved her and wanted her to come to Rimini as soon as he could send her money. Paolo's letters became despairing. 'Why had she not written to him?' 'He loved her so much and begged her, "please write to me Lizzie".'

And then, after a year or so, no more letters came from Paolo. All the letters had been addressed to 'Piper's Farm', the only address that he had for Lizzie.

"What do you think happened?" said Joan. "Why didn't she write back to him? Weren't you allowed to write to a former enemy?"

"I don't know," said Robert. "Perhaps not."

"But his letters came to the farm. Mother kept in touch with Lizzie. Surely she would have forwarded the letters to her. Where did you say Dad found them?"

"In a locked drawer, in Mum's dressing-table."

"How did she come by them?"

"Perhaps she found them when Grandad Piper died and Gran moved in with Great Aunt Elsie. She must have gone to the farm to clear things out before Eileen and Tom moved in."

"Well, why didn't she give them to Lizzie then? Why keep them locked away and why wasn't the birth certificate with the letters?"

"The bureau belonged to Granny Piper," said Robert. "I know Mum brought some pieces of furniture from the farm and you said it was stuck in a groove at the back of the drawer. Perhaps she didn't find it – only the bundle of letters.

Jenny kept a disquieting thought to herself.

Chapter 26

A few weeks after her visit to Robert, the picture of Lizzie and Paolo appeared in the 'Missing and Found' column in the 'Daily Mail' under the 'Missing' heading and in late May a picture of two Land Army girls featured under the 'Found' heading. Philip had managed to pull a few strings and the process of finding Jessie Silverton had been speeded up. Joan was given Jessie's details and when she phoned Susie and told her that Lizzie's wartime friend had been found, she said, "Great. Where does she live? Are you going to see her?"

"Yes. I think I will. She is Mrs. Cummings now. She married one of the soldiers who guarded the prisoners of war, Sergeant Jack Cummings, and they live in a place called Barnsford. Will you come with me to give me some moral support?"

"Yes, of course, I will," Susie said.

Joan wrote to Jessie and Jack Cummings explaining why she had wanted to get in touch with them and asked when it would be convenient to go and see them. Jessie replied, arranging a day and time, saying how much she was looking forward to seeing Joan and Susie and that she would look out some of the wartime photos that she had.

Susie parked her car in the street where Jessie lived and she and Joan found the terraced house and knocked on the door. A spritely, elderly lady opened the door and said, "Hallo. Nice to meet you Miss Lewis. Come in and meet Jack."

She led them along a passage and into a comfortably furnished sitting room, where Jack Cummings was waiting to greet them.

He shook hands with them and said, "Sit down. Make yourselves comfortable."

Jack, who had retained his ability to brew up since his army days, said, "I'll just pop out to the kitchen and put the kettle on."

He saw Susie's eyes look towards Jessie and laughed.

"Jessie couldn't make a decent cup of tea to save her life."

When he was out of earshot, Jessie winked and said, "Why keep a dog and bark yourself? I'm only joking. He's lovely, my Jack."

Jessie had certainly been busy. She had found quite a few photos of her and Lizzie and Joan's mother and her Grandfather and Grandmother Piper as they went about their work on the farm. There was another young man in some of the photos.

"Who is that?" asked Joan.

"That's Ben. His big brother was Mr. Piper's farmhand and when he was called up, Ben came straight from school to take his place. I suppose he'd be about sixteen there. He was a nice boy. Me and Lizzie used to tease him something rotten, but he gave as good as he got."

There were one or two photos cut out of a newspaper and Jessie said that these had been taken for the local 'rag' before the Italian prisoners had been sent home and had included some of the British soldiers as well.

"There, that one. That's Paolo," she said and pointed to a slim handsome young man. "And look. That's my Jack." She called to Jack. "Come and have a look at this."

"Hold on a minute," Jack said. "I'm just coming with the tea."

He settled the tray on a little table, easing the photo album along. "Now then, let's have a cup of tea first and then," looking at Joan, he said, "you can fire away."

Joan wanted to know how Lizzie came to know Paolo.

"There was a British Army camp not far from Mr. Piper's farm and then not long after Lizzie and me came there, it was evacuated and turned into a POW camp. We didn't have anything to do with them at first, but as the war went on and more of the farm labourers were called up, Colonel Brewster, up at the Manor, got some scheme going whereby some of the prisoners helped out at harvest time."

"Yes, that's right," said Jack. "First of all the 'Eyeties' had to stay inside the camp, but when Italy surrendered, regulations eased up a bit and some of them used to go and help at farms in the neighbourhood. Most of them were ordinary blokes, bored stiff in the camp and glad enough to get out and do something."

Susie listened, fascinated that this elderly couple could remember so vividly what had happened all those years ago. She said to Jessie, "Why did you join the Women's Land Army?"

"I fancied myself in the uniform, and my Mum thought it would be a lot less dangerous than being in the ATS or the WAAF."

"How did you meet Lizzie?" asked Joan.

"At the WLA training camp. We only had four weeks' training. I can still remember the look on Mr. Piper's face when he saw us in the farm kitchen that first evening. He must have wondered what he had let himself in for. But we soon got the hang of it. We came in the January of 1942. And was it cold! There used to be ice on the inside of the windows in our bedroom. And we had to get up so early. Six o'clock in the milking shed in the morning and on the go until it was too dark to work and all for £1.8s a week – old money that is. I had never worked so hard in all my life. I had blisters on the palms of my hands as big as half-crowns. Mrs. Piper was a bit on the bossy side, but she really looked after me and Lizzie. And Mrs. Lewis, Anne, was such a lovely young woman. She helped us to settle in and I think with her husband being away in the army, she was glad of a bit of company."

"But Paolo... how did Lizzie come to know him?"

"He was one of the POWs who came to 'Piper's Farm'. He was really nice looking; he had a lovely smile and he was always on hand to give a bit of extra help to Lizzie. We none of us realised how far things had gone until Paolo had gone home. Lizzie was looking a bit peaky, but we all thought that it was because her Mum and Dad had been killed when a buzz bomb fell on their house.

"Then one morning when we came in for breakfast, she passed out. Anne thought something was up and when Lizzie came round, asked her what was the matter. Lizzie said she thought she was having a baby and that it was Paolo's. Anne went and fetched her Mum.

"Mrs. Piper was a bit tight-lipped about it, especially as Paolo had been repatriated by then. 'What's done is done,' she said. 'You had better stay here until the baby is born and then we'll have another think.' I think Lizzie thought that Paolo would write to her and that when the war was over, he would send for her."

"So he never knew about the baby?"

"No. Because Lizzie didn't know where to write to, you see. She was waiting for him to write to her. But he never did. Not a word. Poor Lizzie; she was heartbroken."

'Poor Lizzie,' thought Susie.

"Did she ever tell you or my mother how it happened?"

"No. But I think it must have been about the time the Italians were being sent home. Mr. Piper gave a sort of harvest supper and invited the POWs who had worked on the farm. Jack and another Squaddie were invited too. Ben was there and his brother was home on leave and your mother's cousin Eileen and her Mum and Dad. Quite a family gathering in a way. It would have been easy for Lizzie and Paolo to slip away and be together for the last time."

"What happened after the war?"

"Jack got demobbed and we got married. This photo was taken at our wedding. That's Lizzie. We kept in touch for a while, but you know how it is. We moved a couple of times and we lost touch, but she must have kept in touch with Mrs. Lewis because of the baby."

"How did my mother come to keep me?"

Jessie thought for a moment. "If I remember rightly, just after the war, the government was running one year teacher training courses for returning service personnel. Lizzie was a clever girl and I think that when Paolo didn't make any contact with her, she decided to make the best of a bad job and get on with her life. Yes, that's right; she became a teacher. She left the baby with Mrs. Lewis while she did her training. I suppose it would have been difficult for Lizzie to look after the baby when she finished the course, until she got a job and somewhere to live. She must have come to some arrangement with Mr. and Mrs. Lewis."

"Thank you for being so open with me, Mrs. Cummings. After I found out about the relationship between Lizzie and me, I just wanted to know more about her. You see, I only knew her as Cousin Lizzie."

"I'm sorry Lizzie is dead. We had some good times together."

"Yes. And thank you again."

Joan and a pensive Susie said goodbye to Jessie and Jack Cummings.

"We must keep in touch," Joan said, knowing that she probably wouldn't.

"Why didn't you tell her about the letters?" Susie asked, as they were driving home.

"I don't know. It was all such a long time ago and with Lizzie dead, there didn't seem to be much point."

Chapter 27

Joan went to see her brother and his wife again after the visit to Jessie Cummings to see if he could remember anything else about Cousin Lizzie. Did he know that she had become a teacher? Where had she taught? Had she ever married?

Robert said that he hadn't ever seen much of Lizzie. He knew that their Mother used to see her now and again. Perhaps two or three times a year and that she always went on her own. She never took either of the children with her, nor as far as he could remember did their father accompany her. He didn't think she had married, but he had some vague idea that she had become the headmistress of a girls' school in London. Their father had been a bit reticent about his connection with Lizzie.

But the question of why their mother had kept Paolo's letters from Lizzie remained.

Jenny looked up from reading the letters again.

"I don't suppose we shall ever know the real reason now," she said. "But I think to give you into the care of another person, even though it was a loving one on your mother's part, must have been a very hard decision for Lizzie to make. Perhaps it was just as your father said, that she thought it was in the best interests of you both in the circumstances. As we have seen from Paolo's letters, things were far from settled in Italy at that time. What date is on the first letter?"

"There isn't one," said Joan.

"So we don't know how long it was after he returned home that he wrote."

"Or how long it took for the letter to reach England," said Robert.

"No", said Joan.

"Perhaps Lizzie was already having second thoughts about going to join Paolo and your mother sensed that and so intercepted the letters. I know this has been extremely upsetting for you, Joan, but now that Lizzie has gone too, do you really want to carry it any further?"

Philip wrote to Susie and said that his apartment on the outskirts of Rome was very comfortable and that he was settling into his new post as foreign correspondent for 'The Chronicle'. He would be delighted to have her and Aunt Joan to come and stay with him and what other devious plans had she in mind?

Susie smiled to herself as she read his letter. A trip to Rimini perhaps?

Chapter 28

Philip was waiting for them when Joan and Susie arrived at the Leonardo da Vinci Airport. They had had a good flight, but Joan was glad to be on terra firma once more. Susie was excited to be in Rome again. She and Philip had spent a number of holidays in the city when their father had been attached to the British Embassy there and she was looking forward to taking her aunt on a tour of the historical and cultural attractions that gave Rome its timeless appeal.

Susie and Philip talked animatedly on the short journey to his flat. It was a few months since they had seen each other and Joan, seated in the back of the car, listened to them catching up on the news from home and also the renewal of friendships since Philip had taken up his new appointment.

Philip's flat was on the third floor of an old apartment block and was reached by several flights of stairs. The outer facade of the building hid a very modern interior, so Joan was surprised to find how compact the flat was. It still retained the original high ceilings and large windows and she crossed over to look out of one in the living room. In the hazy light of the late summer evening, the city of Rome was spread out below and beyond that the seven hills on which the ancient city was originally built.

Joan turned to Philip and said, "What a glorious vista."

"Yes. And as you see – all mod cons. Not that far from the bright lights either."

"I'm impressed," said Susie. "How did you wangle this?"

Philip tapped the side of his nose. "I'm not without influence," he said, "and it helps to have contacts in the Embassy who remember Dad."

"Is James Mulholland still there then?"

"The very same."

"Who is James?" enquired Joan

"He was one of the junior secretaries that Dad took under his wing. Took quite a fancy to you, didn't he Suse?"

"Hmm... as I recall, I wasn't the only girl he took a fancy to. He was a bit of a Lothario. Have you seen him lately?"

"Yes. He's still single, so you're in with a chance there."

Philip smiled. As an eighteen year old, Susie had had quite a thing about the handsome James.

Susie returned his smile and shook her head. "He must be what, early thirties now?"

"Yes and still as good looking as ever. I told him you were coming and he said he would like to see you again. I've to phone him and arrange a time and place. I'm sorry Aunt Joan. I'm forgetting my manners. Would you like a drink? Something cool? Tea?"

"A cup of tea would be lovely, please Philip."

"What about you Suse?"

"Yes, tea will be fine."

She followed Philip into his kitchen and he watched while she went round opening all the cupboards, as he knew she would, familiarizing herself with its layout and then returned to the one containing crockery and set out mugs on the breakfast bar.

"Where are we sleeping?"

"Aunt Joan can have my room. You can have the spare room and I'll sleep on the sofa in the sitting room."

They carried the mugs into the living room and as they sat drinking their tea, Philip said, "I thought I'd give you time to unpack a few things and have a rest and then we can go to a trattoria not far from here for dinner."

Joan took her mug and followed Philip as he carried her case into his bedroom.

"Are you sure you want to give up your room, Philip?"

"Yes. Don't worry; it will only be for a few days."

Joan sat on the bed and finished her tea. She felt her eyelids begin to droop and when Susie looked in some minutes later, she found her aunt sound asleep.

"Have you any idea what Aunt Joan wants to do, Suse?"

"Are you going to be able to get time off while we're here?"

"I've got to work until Friday and then I've got a week off."

"I know the real purpose of this visit is to go to Rimini, but I thought if we could stay here with you for a few days, we could take her to see something of Rome first."

"She does want to go to Rimini, doesn't she? You're not pushing her are you?"

"No, Philip. I'm not. Mum asked her if she really wanted to carry it further now that Lizzie has gone too, but she really does want to find Paolo, or at least members of his family if that is possible. Finding out about Lizzie and Paolo was quite upsetting for her you know and I think she just wants to settle her own feelings about it all. I thought if we could go with her, it might make it easier for her. She has always been so kind to us. It's the least we can do."

"Yes, you're right. We'll talk about it over dinner tonight. Do you want to shower first, or shall I?"

"You go first; I'll unpack and then go and wake Aunt Joan."

They walked the short distance to the trattoria, where Philip had become a regular patron since moving into the district. The proprietario, Enrico, welcomed Signor Lewis and his bella signore and showed them to Philip's usual table. He paid effusive attention to Joan and Susie, advising them on their choice of dishes, and made much of showing

Philip the wine list, knowing that he always chose the house wine. An amused Philip sat back and watched Enrico exuding charm for the benefit of his aunt and his sister. A delighted Susie lapped it up. Joan took a more reserved stance. Enrico's attention to the English party paid off. They had a delightful meal and he got a larger tip than usual.

On his way into his office the next morning, Philip took Joan and Susie to a bus stop in the centre of Rome, from where they could catch a bus to the Vatican City. He arranged a place to meet them later in the day and waved them off with a cheery "Have fun."

Before catching the bus to the Piazza del Risorgimento, Susie stopped at a newsstand and bought two three-day city passes, which gave them access to the public transport system and free admission to the first two museums or sites visited and reduced tickets and discounts for further museums. She also bought a map of the city.

"That seems like a good buy," said Joan.

"Yes. Even though we shall only be here for two days, it's still worth the fifteen Euros."

As they rode through the city, Susie pointed out various places to Joan.

"You're very knowledgeable, Susie."

"Yes, Mum used to take us somewhere different nearly every day. Rather like when we came to stay with you in London."

"Only your mother?"

"Yes. Dad was usually tied up at the Embassy."

"Didn't he ever take time off when you came on holiday?"

"Sometimes. One of these days I'm going to take time out and do the 'Grand Tour'. We're here. Do you want a guided tour, or shall we take our time and just wander round?"

"Let's buy a guide from the kiosk and take our time."

Joan was glad that she had made that decision, as she told Philip later, when they sat drinking a glass of wine in one of the small bars situated around the perimeters of the Piazza Navon.

"There was so much to see Philip. Susie bought us three-day city passes, but really it would take a lot longer than three days to do justice to the places we have been to today. When we stood in the vast Piazza San Pietro and looked towards the great church of St. Peter, it was awesome, but inside the beauty of the paintings took my breath away. Everything was so magnificent, it was overwhelming. We stood for ages gazing up at the painted ceiling of the Sistine Chapel."

"What impressed you most?"

"The Michelangelo Pieta and the great bronze Baldacchino by Bernini – the statues of the saints in the piazza. I don't know. The treasures in the Vatican Museum that we visited; the beautiful Vatican Gardens. Just about everything."

"And tomorrow," said Susie, "the ancient monuments – the 'centro historica'."

Philip smiled at his aunt's enthusiasm. "You enjoyed your day then?"

"Oh yes. I'm glad we decided to stay in Rome for a few days. Today has been a marvellous experience and I'm really looking forward to tomorrow. All this sightseeing has made me ravenous. Where are you taking us tonight Philip?"

"What about an authentic pizza?" said Susie. "Then afterwards we can find a gelateria."

"Pizza and ice cream suit you, Aunty?" said Philip.

"Pizza and ice cream would suit me fine."

They walked through the gathering dusk to Da Francesco in the Piazza del Fico. Eating pizza was another novel experience for Joan and she enjoyed the cheerful atmosphere in the traditional pizzeria and was delighted when a guitar strumming busker entertained them as they sat outside waiting to be served.

"I think I need a walk before I can even contemplate an ice cream," Joan said to Susie while they waited for Philip to settle the bill.

"By the time we get to the Gelateria della Parma and see what's on offer, I guarantee even you will be tempted," said Susie. "It's the best ice cream I've ever tasted."

"Any gelateria sells the best ice cream you have ever tasted," said her brother.

"That's true."

Driving home to Philip's apartment, Joan was happy and relaxed. Having the children with her on this search for Paolo Cardi had been a good idea.

"I phoned James yesterday," said Philip on the way into the city the next day. "He's invited us out to dinner tonight, so I think the best thing would be for you to meet me back at the flat after you have seen as much of the 'centro historica' as you want to. That will give you time for a rest and to get changed."

"Where is he taking us?" asked Susie.

"He didn't say. Just to meet him by the Spanish Steps at about seven o'clock. Don't overdo it today and try to keep out of the sun, or you'll get a red nose," Philip teased. "See you later."

Susie was mindful of Philip's teasing remark. She certainly didn't want to meet James with a sunburnt nose.

Before they set out for the tourist attractions, Susie and Joan enjoyed a cappuccino sitting outside at a cafe while they decided where to begin. Susie consulted the map.

"All the ancient monuments are pretty well within walking distance from each other," she said. "If we start off with the Colosseum I think we'll manage to see most of them before we make our way back to the flat. Ready then?"

Susie was a competent guide but when, as sometimes happened, they were caught up in the inevitable groups of tourists being given a guided tour, they did eavesdrop. They had been listening to a guide expounding the violent history of the Colosseum as they stood in the ruins of its amphitheatre and Joan turned to Susie and said, "These buildings still have echoes of the past, don't they?"

"Yes. I can just see Androcles preparing to defend himself against the lion."

"Oh Susie. Do you remember me telling that story to you and Philip?"

"Yes, I do. I remember thinking about it the very first time I came here." And espying a 20th century gladiator, she said, "Let's have our photo taken with that Russell Crowe look-a-like, shall we?"

"The Forum next, I think," said Susie, "then we'll go to the Campo di Fieri and find a place to have some lunch. We can leave the Trevi Fountain until this evening. It looks magical when it is floodlit and if we are meeting James by the Spanish Steps, we can leave that until later too. That leaves the Pantheon and then we'll make our way back to the flat."

They entered the Forum by way of the Arco di Tito and Joan followed Susie into the square where the Senators of ancient Rome had conducted the affairs of the day. She stopped and looked around her, trying to imagine what it would have been like when it was alive with people and the Temple of Castor and Pollux was more than the three columns that were all that remained of the once important building. And the broken statues? Who were they? Had Mark Anthony actually stood on that ruined Rostrum? What had happened to the gleaming white marble law courts?

Susie was consulting the guide book. "It says here that it wasn't marauding barbarians, but the Romans themselves who plundered it for building materials in medieval times."

Joan stood a little while longer taking it all in, waiting for Susie to finish taking photographs, before they moved on to the Campo di Fiori. They found a cafe and sat outside to eat and Joan remarked on the scaffolding that surrounded some of the buildings that they had passed.

"They are probably cleaning the buildings in preparation for the Millennium Celebrations."

"Yes, of course. I hadn't thought of that."

"Shall we be on our way then?"

Susie, seeing the Pantheon again after six years, was just as awestruck as her aunt.

"Every time I came to Rome, I always came here. Each time I see it, I find it more fascinating."

They stood looking at the stupendous marble columns supporting the triangular pediment.

"It is certainly impressive," said Joan.

"Wait until you see inside."

If the outside was impressive, the interior was more so. Joan gasped as she looked up at the perfect semi-sphere of the dome, lit by a nine metre oculus (round window) which was meant to be a symbolic connection between the temple and the Gods.

"It's amazing," she said, "and so well preserved."

"Yes. That's mainly because it was consecrated as a church in AD 606. Even so, it didn't entirely escape some plundering. Do you remember that huge bronze Baldacchino in St. Peter's? That was made from bronze filched from the Pantheon's ceiling cladding. But at least they didn't melt down the Roman doors."

"They wouldn't be allowed to do that today, would they? Someone would slap a preservation order on it."

"Times were different then. Think of all the buildings that have been allowed to fall down at home."

"Yes indeed."

"Shall we make our way back to the flat?"

"Yes. I must say I could do with putting my feet up for a while. But I've had a wonderful day, Susie. Thank you so much for sharing it with me."

"We'll have quite an interesting evening as well, if I know James."

CHAPTER 29

Susie dressed very carefully that evening. She chose a halter-necked black silk dress, splashed with white flowers. The bodice was fitted and the full skirt came to just below her knees. Her black strappy sandals matched the clutch bag which carried the few necessities to see her through the evening. Her dark blonde hair was caught back at the nape of her neck with a diamante clip and a black silk stole, should she need to cover her bare shoulders, completed her elegant ensemble. When she came out of the spare bedroom and into the living room, Philip said, "Wow!"

"Thank you Philip." And giving a pirouette said, "I'll do then?"

"I should say so."

He was dressed casually in a pair of well pressed beige chinos and a light blue cotton open-necked shirt under a beige linen jacket. Their aunt wore a simple plum coloured silk sleeveless shift with a matching jacket. She regarded her niece and nephew affectionately.

"I think we are ready to dine wherever James has decided to take us," she said.

She looked very carefully at the unusually elegant Susie. 'Who was this – James?'

Philip parked the car in a quiet side street and they made their way towards the Spanish Steps. James was already waiting there and Susie's heart flipped at the sight of his tall, slim figure immaculately dressed in a light grey summer suit and white open-necked silk shirt.

'For heaven's sake,' she told herself. 'You are an up and coming young lawyer, not some gauche eighteen year old.'

James saw them and came towards Philip, his hand outstretched.

"Hello Philip. Good to see you again."

Philip introduced James to his aunt.

"This is my aunt, Miss Lewis, and of course, you know Susie."

"How do you do Miss Lewis? Susan, delighted to meet you again." 'Absolutely,' he thought.

"Hallo James." 'Still a smooth operator' thought Susie. 'He was the only one to still call her Susan.'

"I've booked a table at 'The Forum' for eight-thirty. Time for us to stroll there and have a drink in the bar before we dine."

He offered his arm to Joan and led the way. Susie and Philip, following behind them, grinned at each other. Still the same old James. He could charm the birds out of the trees.

James led them into the bar of 'The Forum Hotel' and ordered drinks. They chatted pleasantly about nothing particular. Joan wondered how much Philip had told James about the purpose of her visit to Italy but James, ever the diplomat, said nothing. They took the lift to the restaurant on the rooftop terrace and admired the stunning view of Rome at night.

The food and the service at 'The Forum' was a far cry from Enrico's cosy trattoria and Susie was glad she had dressed to kill. James was solicitous towards Joan, asking how she was enjoying her visit to Rome and on hearing that they planned to visit Perugia on the way to Rimini, suggested that they stay at a charming hotel, 'The Brufani Palace', in the centre of the town.

Susie told James that her aunt had not yet visited the Trevi Fountain.

"You can't miss that," he said. "We'll walk there after dinner. You know the tradition of throwing coins into the fountain?"

"Yes," said Susie, looking straight at him. "You took me there the last time I was in Rome."

"So I did."

James slipped Susie's arm through his when they left the hotel. Philip offered his arm to Joan and they smiled at James' obvious ploy.

Joan was glad they had left the visit to the Trevi Fountain until nightfall. Floodlit, it was as Susie had said – magical.

"What do I have to do?" asked Joan.

"You close your eyes, throw a coin into the fountain and make a wish," said Susie.

"And does your wish come true, Susie?"

"Not always," she replied.

"Try again Susan," James said, handing her a coin. "This time it might."

Susie looked at the coin and then at James. She closed her eyes and tossed it to join the hundreds of others in the fountain and remembered the last time James had given her a one lira coin and the wish she had made.

They took turns to throw coins into the fountain, all except James. He was determined that he would make his wish come true, without leaving it to chance.

"Thank you so much James," said Joan. "It has been a lovely evening." She shook hands with him. "I hope we shall meet again."

"I hope so too."

"Thanks for dinner James. We're making an early start in the morning. I'll call you when we get back."

"Yes, you do that." And the two young men shook hands again.

"Goodnight James. Thanks for dinner."

"Goodnight Susan. We must meet again before you go back home," and he kissed her softly on both cheeks and then briefly on her mouth.

James stood looking after them as they made their way back to where Philip had left his car. Susie knew he was waiting for her to turn and wave and with the taste of his kiss still on her lips, it took all of her strength of will not to.

Chapter 30

Early the next morning Philip found the telephone number of the 'Brufani Palace Hotel' and phoned to see if he could make a reservation. He mentioned James' name to the receptionist, who recognised it immediately. Philip waited while the girl checked the hotel reservations.

"Signor Lewis, we can only accommodate your party for two days."

"That's OK. Two days will be fine. We are just passing through on our way to Rimini. We are coming from Rome and should arrive some time this afternoon."

"Thank you, signor. Your rooms will be ready for you."

Philip had planned the route to Perugia to bypass as many of the main roads as possible; instead they travelled through the beautiful, rugged countryside of Umbria by winding roads that led them through medieval hill towns, sloping farmlands and past vineyards and olive groves.

They stopped for lunch at an inn in a small village on the way to Perugia. The fare was very basic; flat bread brushed with olive oil and garlic, cheese, slices of cured ham, fat ripe tomatoes and glasses of the local wine. The dialect was a little difficult for Philip to understand, but the innkeeper was delighted at his attempts to order what was, in effect, the equivalent of a 'ploughman's lunch' in his 'city' Italian.

Sitting outside at the back of the inn on a terrace overlooking the countryside, Joan said, "What a contrast from yesterday. Rome was bustling with energy. This place is so peaceful; their way of life can't have changed much in centuries."

They reached Perugia in the late afternoon and Philip stopped to enquire the whereabouts of the 'Brufani Palace Hotel' and was directed to the Piazza Italia in the centre of the town. He drove onto the forecourt and got out of the car and went to the reception desk to confirm their reservations. He came back to the car with a porter, who carried their luggage into the hotel, where they collected the keys to their rooms.

Joan and Susie were shown into an impeccably decorated twin-bedded room with views over the spectacular countryside. Philip's room was at the front of the hotel and looked out over the piazza. Before unpacking, he crossed the hallway and in answer to his knock, Susie opened their door. He went in and looked around him before asking, "What do you think of it?"

"It's really rather grand isn't it," said Joan.

Susie picked up a brochure from the dressing-table.

"'The Brufani Palace Hotel' retains much of its original charm and character," she read. "It is famous for its intimate elegant atmosphere and traditional hospitality – and listen to this – it also has a sauna, a fitness centre, a Turkish Bath AND a subterranean pool situated over Estruscan ruins. Trust James to know of a place like this. Pity we're only here for two days."

"The receptionist said there is a private car park here. She says the town is quite compact and to leave the car and either walk or use the public transport. We can leave our unpacking until later. I'll go and park the car and then we can have a wander round."

"OK. We'll wait for you on the forecourt."

There were tables and chairs set out under sunshades, so Susie and Joan sat down to wait for Philip. A waiter came to the table and asked if there was anything he could do for them. Susie ordered glasses of spremuta di limone. The drink came in tall frosted glasses and was sharply refreshing.

Presently Philip returned with some leaflets and sat down at the table. Susie passed a glass of the lemonade to him.

"I'm glad you ordered one for me." He took a sip. "This is absolutely delicious. I've been talking to the receptionist again. No wonder James comes here so often. There seems to be some kind of festival or trade fair every week and there are any number of museums. Have a look at these," he said, passing some of the leaflets to Susie and his aunt. "It appears to be quite a cultural centre and with James being the Cultural Attaché at the Embassy, he would know about these events."

"And being the Cultural Attaché, he would stay in the best hotel, wouldn't he?" said Susie wryly.

"Knowing James, yes."

Philip swallowed the last of his drink. "Shall we go and have a look round then?"

They walked out of the Piazza Italia and down steep, narrow streets, through small squares, until they came to the centre of Perugia, the Piazza IV Novembre. In the centre of the square was the Fontana Maggiore, which seemed to be the main attraction, and they joined the crowds of tourists and students to admire what was reputed to be the oldest piece of bronze casting to survive from the middle ages.

Philip said, "We really only have this evening and tomorrow to explore this place. How much sightseeing do you want to do?"

"I hadn't realised there would be so much to see," said Joan. "I thought it would be just a small provincial town. A stopover on the way to Rimini."

"Let's find the tourist information bureau and get a guide book, otherwise we could wander around aimlessly and miss the really interesting sights," Susie said. "I'd like to find out more about that fountain and why the piazza is called the IV Novembre."

"How far is Assisi from here?" asked Joan. "I would like to go there if possible."

"We could always go there on the way back to Rome," Philip replied.

As the hotel receptionist had said, the town was quite compact and in the tourist information office they found a 'walk around Perugia' type booklet, which listed the major buildings, art galleries and museums, with a short summary of facts concerning each one. That settled, they strolled from one piazza to another in a roundabout way, until they found themselves at the foot of the scala mobile (escalator) which took them back to the Piazza Italia and they returned to the hotel to bathe and change for dinner.

After dinner, as they sat out on the lamplit terrace planning the next day's sightseeing, the sound of music drifted up to the hotel and Susie and Philip decided to return to the Piazza IV Novembre to listen to the student buskers who congregated there, playing guitars and drums for their own and the tourists' amusement.

Joan said she was quite comfortable sitting where she was, looking through the leaflets again, and declined their invitation to join them.

She was glad to have some time to herself. The last few days had been quite hectic and she had hardly had time to consider what awaited her when she arrived in Rimini. She hoped that she would find a satisfactory conclusion to the unexpected part of Cousin Lizzie's legacy. Joan yawned, suddenly tired, and went up to her room to prepare for bed.

There was a stillness about the Sunday morning, broken only by the sound of church bells calling the faithful to worship, and after a leisurely breakfast Joan, Susie and Philip made their way once again to the Piazza IV Novembre, as a starting point to begin their tour of Perugia. They had decided that rather than try to visit all the tourist attractions, they would each choose one that was of particular interest to them, but before doing so, they took a closer look at the Fontana Maggiore.

They walked round the fountain trying to identify, from the description in the guide book, the principal features of the two polygonal basins which had white marble bas-reliefs depicting episodes from the Old Testament, classical myths, Aesop's Fables and the twelve months of the year and were crowned by a group of three bronze water nymphs sculpted by Giovanni. They admired the carefully conceived decorative scheme designed to illustrate the city's glory and achievements, of what was considered to be the oldest piece of bronze casting to survive from the Middle Ages.

"A thing of beauty is a joy forever," quoted Joan. "And this fountain is certainly a thing of beauty."

"I've found a bit about the piazza," said Susie, reading from the guide book. "It says 'the Piazza Grande was built in 1224, but there are two schools of thought about when the name was changed to Piazza IV Novembre. One says that it was after the referendum in 1861, when Umbria joined the newly formed Kingdom of Italy when Victor Emmanul II of Sardinia was proclaimed king, and the other says it could have been after the unification of Italy after World War I.' So you pays your money and you takes your choice," said Susie.

"That's a bit disappointing isn't it?" said Joan. "You would have thought a guide book would get it right."

"Typical," said Philip. "Shall we move on?"

He was quite happy to saunter behind Susie as they explored the sequence of magnificent rooms of the Palazzo dei Priori, some of them still used for public meetings. Being a lawyer, Susie was particularly interested in the Saladei Notari, with ceiling frescos that dated from the end of the thirteenth century. Philip dutifully followed his aunt around the Cathedral San Lorenzo, whose architecture, while not especially striking, had a strangely comforting feel about the homely gloom of the place, lit only by a cluster of candles in front of the altar, or by the feeble glimmer of daylight filtering through the stained glass windows. But he really wanted to get back to the hotel and take advantage of the fitness centre and the swimming pool.

It being Sunday, many of the historic buildings closed before one o'clock, so after they had stopped for a light lunch at a cafe in the pedestrianized Corso Vannucci, he left them to wander round the antiques' market in the tiny Giardini Carducci at the southern end of the Corso Vannucci. The gardens stood atop the once massive sixteenth century fortress known as the Rocco Paolino and had lovely views looking out over the countryside. In the ruins of the Rocco, they found an art exhibition taking place and spent a pleasant hour or so browsing round before returning to their hotel. Susie went to find Philip and joined him in the swimming pool. Joan sat out on the terrace of the hotel with a pot of 'English tea', thinking how best to approach Paolo Cardi if he was still alive.

Susie and Philip came to join her on the terrace for a pre-dinner drink and seeing his aunt sitting thoughtfully sipping her Campari and soda, Philip said, "Are you sure you want to continue to Rimini, Aunt Joan?"

"Yes. You see, besides leaving me the money, when I went to see Lizzie's solicitor, he gave me this," and from her handbag she took out a small chamois leather purse. She loosened the strings and drew out a gold St. Christopher medallion on a thin gold chain. On the back was an inscription in Italian. She had some idea of what it might mean, but she gave the medallion to Philip for him to translate.

"It says 'God keep you safe'. Whose is it?"

"I believe it belongs to Paolo. He must have given it to Lizzie before he was repatriated and if he is still alive, I think I should return it to him."

CHAPTER 31

The journey to Rimini the next day took them through the now familiar terrain of the Umbrian countryside, until they reached the coastal road that took them to their destination. They checked in at a small hotel in Rimini that catered for travellers who wished to make it a base for exploring the Adriatic Coast. The rooms were small, but comfortably furnished, and there was a trattoria which adjoined the main part of the hotel and provided food characteristic of the area.

After they had settled in, they took the short walk down to the beach from where they could see the yachts moored in the Marina Centro. Looking around her, Joan thought how different her life would have been had Lizzie taken her and gone to join Paolo. Susie had taken her sandals off and gone to paddle in the sea. Philip turned to his aunt and said, "We could walk along the beach until we reach the marina if you like."

"Yes. Now that I'm here, I feel a little uncertain. I do want to find Paolo, but I don't want to cause him any distress after all this time."

"You don't have to make actual contact unless you want to."

"No. I know. Let's join Susie for a paddle. Perhaps there will be a bar along the promenade and we can have a drink there. I feel the need for some 'Dutch courage'."

They walked along the water's edge until they came to a flight of steps which led them up onto the promenade lined with bars, cafes and restaurants. Dusting the sand from their feet and replacing their sandals, they walked along until they came to a likely looking bar with tables set out on a terrace and sat down.

A young waitress came to take their order and hearing them speak, said in slightly accented English, "Can I help you to decide what you would like to drink?"

They looked up in surprise and Philip said, "What do you suggest?"

"Something long and cool. I can recommend my father's special cocktail."

"Thank you. We'll try that then."

"Have you seen the name above the lintel?" said Susie when the girl had gone back inside the bar.

Joan squinted in the light reflected off the sea. "I can't see."

"It says Proprietorio Vincente Cardi. Perhaps we could ask her about Paolo."

"Gently does it, Susie," said Philip.

Susie held up her hands in a defensive manner. "I'll leave it to you Philip. Your Italian is better than mine."

The Cardi Special was delicious and when the girl came back to clear a nearby table, Philip asked her for the bill. She seemed eager to practise her English and asked them how far they had come.

"We are on a touring holiday. We have come from Perugia today, but we've been in Rome. We're just going where the fancy takes us," said Philip.

The girl looked puzzled. She did not understand what the phrase 'where the fancy takes us' meant.

"Ah yes," she said, still not quite sure what it meant, as Philip, seeing her puzzlement, tried to explain to her in Italian.

"You speak well, signor."

"Thank you." Then he said, "We have friends in England who asked us to look up a man they knew a long time ago. His name was Paolo Cardi and he came from Rimini. He was a prisoner of war and worked on our great-grandfather's farm. Our friends lost touch with him after the war. It's just a chance that he is still alive, but they would like to be remembered to him. We understand that his father kept a trattoria on the sea front before the war."

"Yes I see. One moment please. I will ask my father."

"Papa… there are English people outside asking for Nonno. They know he was a prisoner of war in England."

Vincente Cardi stood behind the bar and looked out at the group of people sitting outside. "Why do they want to see him after all this time?"

"I don't know. The man speaks Italian. Perhaps you should go and speak to him."

"Buona sera, signor. My daughter says you are looking for Signor Paolo Cardi. Who is enquiring after him?"

"A Mr. and Mrs. Jack Cummings. Sergeant Cummings was a guard at the prisoner of war camp in Elmersdale and Mrs. Cummings, Jessie, also worked at 'Piper's Farm' during the war. We had occasion to meet them recently and, as I was saying, when they heard we were coming to Rimini, they told us about Paolo and wanted to be remembered to him, if he is still alive."

"Are you staying long in Rimini, signor?"

"Just two or three days."

"I will make enquiries for you and if you come tomorrow, I may have news of him."

"Thank you. That is most kind of you. I must say I enjoyed your special cocktail."

"Yes. It was absolutely delicious," said Susie smiling at him.

Vincente Cardi looked at the older English woman, when she too thanked him. There was something vaguely familiar about her.

"That was sneaky of you, Philip," said his sister.

"You're not the only devious one in the family. If his name is Cardi, he might be a relation of Paolo's. When I mentioned 'Piper's Farm', that seemed to ring a bell."

"You can understand his being wary. They probably want to protect Paolo. He must be an old man now," said Joan.

"Well nothing more can be done until tomorrow. What say we walk along to the end of the promenade and then return to the hotel?" said Philip.

As they walked along, Susie noticed that more than one bar or restaurant had the name 'Cardi' alongside 'proprietori'.

"I think we may well find Paolo," she said "and probably members of his family too."

It was towards the end of the season and Vincente's bar was quiet that evening.

"Paoli," he called to his son. "Come and look after the bar. I am going to see Nonno. Carmela, take off your apron and come with me."

They walked along the promenade, passing the time of day with friends and relatives, as they made their way to the Trattoria Marina, where they found Paolo sitting outside sipping a glass of wine.

"Buona sera Padre. How are you?"

"Buona sera Vincente. I am well. And you? Carmela, how lovely to see you," he said, as she came to kiss him, and to Vincente, "What brings you here at this time of day? Business not so good?"

"Well, you know how it is at the end of the season. It was a bit quiet tonight."

"Yes, yes. It is quiet here tonight also."

"Carmela; tell your grandfather about the English visitors."

"Three English people came to the bar this evening, Nonno. A young man, who spoke quite good Italian, and two women – one young and one about Papa's age. I thought I would practise my English and they were very pleasant. Then they said that they had friends who had asked them to look for a man they knew a long time ago in the war. This man was called Paolo Cardi and he had worked on their great-grandfather's farm when he was a prisoner of war. I think they meant you, Nonno."

"There are other Paolo Cardis in Rimini."

"Yes, but the young man said that these friends were called Cummings and that the husband had been a sergeant guarding prisoners of war at 'Piper's Farm' and that the wife was called Jessie."

"Jessie? Not Lizzie?"

"No. Jessie and Jack I think. The young man said that these people wished to be remembered to you. Do you remember them Nonno?"

"It was a long time ago, but yes, I remember Sergeant Cummings and Jessie too and Mr. and Mrs. Piper – the farmer and his wife. They were kind to the prisoners who worked for them. Well, you can tell them, if they come to the bar again, that you have told me."

"I think they would like to tell you themselves, Padre. Perhaps they would like to take back a message from you."

"Yes, perhaps."

"We can't make it too obvious that we are anxious to meet Signor Cardi," said Philip. "It's lovely here and I wouldn't mind spending some time on the beach."

"Yes, I think I'd like to do that too," said Joan. "We've had quite a taxing week and it would be nice to sit and swim and relax."

"That's fine by me," Susie agreed. "The sun is still quite strong, so perhaps we should see if we can hire a sunshade. We can have a lazy day tomorrow and then go to Vincente's bar in the evening. Do you think he will tell us, even if he does know Paolo Cardi?"

Carmela was looking out for the English tourists and when they came to the bar the next evening, she went over to them to take their order.

"Buona sera," she said. "Have you had a pleasant day?"

"Yes," replied Philip. "We have spent the day relaxing on the beach."

"What would like to drink?"

"Three of your father's specials please."

Carmela went back inside the bar and spoke to her father.

"What shall I say? Shall I say that we know the Paolo Cardi they are looking for?"

"Yes, I think we can say that we know of him. Let them finish their drinks and then go with them and take them to meet your grandfather."

Carmela took the drinks to their table and said, "There is a man called Paolo Cardi who keeps a trattoria at the end of the promenade. My father says perhaps this is the man you are looking for. I can take you to meet him if you wish."

"That's very kind of you. It would be great if he is the man our friends knew," Philip said.

"When you have finished your drinks, I will take you."

"I'm pretty sure she knows he is the one we are looking for," said Susie. "Her father looks very like that photograph of Paolo as a young man."

"Yes, I thought that," said Joan.

They finished their drinks and Carmela came to clear the table. "One moment please," she said.

As they walked towards the Trattoria Marina, people greeted Carmela. Some of the young men called out teasing comments to her. "Hey Carmela. Who's your new sweetheart?"

She smiled and waved her hand at them. "Pay them no attention."

They found Signor Cardi sitting outside his trattoria. Carmela went to him and kissed him on both cheeks.

"Buona sera, Nonno," she said. I have brought the English visitors to meet you."

She turned to Philip. "This is my grandfather, Signor Paolo Cardi. Please introduce yourselves to him."

"Good evening sir. I'm Philip Lewis. This is my aunt, Joan Lewis, and my sister, Susan Lewis."

The elderly man rose to his feet and shook hands with them.

"Carmela, go inside and bring glasses and a bottle of wine."

'He was still a handsome man,' thought Joan. 'The shock of dark hair was now iron grey, the tall figure thickened, but behind his gold rimmed spectacles, the brown eyes, so like her own, were still bright. Did he see any resemblance to Lizzie in her? Did he see any resemblance to himself? But then he didn't know the relationship between them, so perhaps not.'

"Please sit down and tell me how you come to know Sergeant Cummings. Carmela, pour our guests a glass of wine."

"When our grandmother died, our grandfather found some photos in a bureau that had been our great-grandmother's. They were of our great-grandparents, Mr. and Mrs. Piper, and our grandmother, Anne Lewis, and two Land Army girls who worked at 'Piper's Farm' during the war. One photo was of a group of people, another was of a girl called Lizzie, arm in arm with a young man in an unfamiliar uniform, and another photo, cut out of the local newspaper, the 'Elmersdale Gazette', was of a group of Italian prisoners of war, taken before they were repatriated, and the British soldiers who guarded them. Our grandmother, Anne, had kept in touch with Lizzie and we were curious to know who the other people in the photos were, so we put an advertisement in the 'Daily Mail', one of our national newspapers, and we had a reply from Mrs. Jessie Cummings. My aunt and my sister went to see Jessie, who had married Sergeant Cummings, and she told us about the other people in the photos. She said that the young man with Lizzie was an Italian prisoner of war called Paolo Cardi and that he came from Rimini. I work on a newspaper in Rome and when my aunt told Jessie that she and my sister were coming to visit me, she said that if we went to Rimini and happened to find Paolo, to give him their best regards and remember the good times you all had when you worked together on the farm. Of course, we said we would, but we really did not think that we would actually find the Paolo in the photo. We've brought the photos with us. Would you like to see them?" Philip finished.

Signor Cardi, who had been listening intently to Philip, took the photos and looked at them.

"Yes. I am the Paolo Cardi in the photos. Thank you for coming to give me their message. You may tell them I was pleased to receive it and that I am still alive and well in Rimini. Some more wine?"

Carmela looked at her grandfather and then at the English people.

"What a strange story,' she thought. And 'What peculiar people the English were.'

"He didn't give much away did he?" Susie said when they had taken their leave of Signor Cardi and were walking back to their hotel. "And he never mentioned Lizzie, did he?"

"No, he didn't. But I think he must know that that is not the whole story," said Joan. "Do you think he noticed any likeness in me to him or Lizzie?"

"Well, he certainly kept looking at you all the time Philip was telling him the story. And the girl, Carmela, I wonder what she made of it?"

Philip said, "How do you feel now that you have met Paolo, Aunt Joan?"

"As to feelings, I don't really know, but then I don't know how I feel about Lizzie either. They are both so far removed from my real life. He's not as old as I thought he would be and he is still a handsome man."

"Handsome!" said Susie. "He must have been drop dead gorgeous when he was young. No wonder Lizzie fell for him."

"Oh Susie," said her aunt, laughing. "You are incorrigible."

Carmela cleared the glasses from the table and came to sit with her Grandfather.

"You are not unhappy that I brought the English people to visit you, Nonno?"

"No, no, cara mia. It was a kind thought. As you say, they were very pleasant and the young man does speak well."

"Buona notte Carmela," he said, as she came to kiss him goodbye.

"Buona notte Nonno."

"Well, what happened?" her father said when Carmela reached home.

"It was a very strange story, but Nonno was not unhappy that I took them to meet him. He seemed pleased that their friends remembered him after all this time. They showed him some photos of him and the farmer and his wife and other people and in one, Nonno was standing arm in arm with a very pretty girl called Lizzie, I think."

Chapter 32

"What are you two doing today?" asked Joan. "Swimming and sunbathing again?"

"When we were walking along the promenade yesterday, I noticed that one tour operator runs a day cruise to Venice from the Marina. How about that?" said Philip. "If we get a move on we might just catch it."

"Just the day for a trip round the lighthouse," said Susie.

The cruise ship took them across the Lagoon of Venice and as they disembarked, there were tour guides plying their trade to take them on a guided tour of Venice. They opted for the two-hour tour, which took in St. Mark's Square and its Basilica, the Doge's Palace and the Bridge of Sighs and left them time to take a trip on a gondola, before going back to the ship. Included in the cruise was a tour of the Lagoon's nearby islands of Murano, Burano and Torcello to view the colourful houses, picturesque squares and to visit the famous glass blowing factory and purchase mementoes of their trip.

Sailing back to the Marina Centro, they all agreed it had been a very full, but interesting day. Susie and Philip decided to go and explore the old town of Rimini, before going back to the hotel. Joan said that she wanted to go and see Paolo again and return his medallion.

"Are you sure you don't want us to come with you?" asked Susie.

"Yes, quite sure. I would rather go on my own," replied Joan.

"I thought you would come again," Paolo said in halting, accented English when Joan greeted him, before sitting down to join him at a table outside the Trattoria Marina.

Joan looked at him in surprise. She had come prepared with an English/Italian dictionary.

"I learnt some English in the camp and, as you know, my grand-daughter speaks English. It is good for business."

"What my nephew told you yesterday wasn't the whole story."

"I know. How is Lizzie?"

"She died last year."

"I am sorry to hear that."

"Among other things, she left me this."

Joan took the medallion from its chamois purse and gave it to Paolo. He took it from her and turned it over in his hand.

"My mother gave it to me when I had to join the army and I gave it to Lizzie as a love token before I was sent home. What happened? Why did she not answer my letters?"

"She never received your letters. My mother, Anne Lewis, found them in her mother's bureau after she died and by then Lizzie had given up hope of joining you and so she put the past behind her and got on with her life. She became a teacher, but she never married."

"Why did she leave you the medallion?"

"Because I was her daughter and, until recently, I didn't know that. I was brought up to believe I was Anne and Edward Lewis' child. When Anne died, I inherited her mother's bureau and it was then that I found my birth certificate and the photo of you and Lizzie in an envelope hidden at the back of the bureau drawer. That is when I contacted Jessie to find out who the young man with Lizzie was. Jessie told me that Lizzie was very much in love with you and that she was heartbroken when she thought you had forgotten her."

"I never forgot Lizzie. I thought she had changed her mind. Like her I had to get on with my life. I had no idea that she carried my child. You have met my son Vincente. I have another son, Paolo and a daughter, Elisabetta. My wife is away visiting her and her new baby boy; otherwise you would have met her. You are like Lizzie, but you are also like my Elisabetta."

"I hope I have not caused you distress. I didn't want to do that, but I did want to meet you and return your medallion," Joan said.

Paolo took hold of Joan's hand, placed the medallion in it and closed her fingers over it.

"I'm glad that you came. I would like you to take the medallion as a keepsake from me as well as Lizzie. Perhaps a glass of wine before we part?"

"Thank you. Tomorrow we must begin our journey back to Rome and then home to England. I'm glad that I came to Italy. It is a beautiful country. And I am happy to have met you."

They finished their wine and stood up to shake hands, but then by some mutual instinct, they embraced each other.

"Arrevederci Joan."

"Goodbye Paolo."

Walking through the cobbled streets of Rimini's old quarter, Susie said to Philip, "Do you think we should have gone with Aunt Joan to see Paolo again?"

"No. I think they both needed to see each other alone. He knew there was more to the tale than I told him. Seeing Paolo and Aunt Joan together, even I could see the similarities between them."

"Do you think they will keep in touch now that they have met?"

"I don't know Suse. We'll have to wait and see. And no probing. Let Aunt Joan tell us what happened in her own good time. Right!"

"Right."

CHAPTER 33

As Assisi came into view, the visual impact of the city perched half-way up Monte Subasio, its pink and white marble buildings shimmering in the midday sunlight, was amazing.

"Can we stop for a moment Philip?" said Joan.

Philip stopped the car and they all got out and stood by the roadside.

"This must be the most beautiful view I have seen since coming to Italy," said Joan. "I think it was worth breaking our journey back to Romc to visit it, don't you?"

From the field of poppies immediately in front of them, the landscape unfolded; houses appeared through tiers of wooded areas that wound upward to the skyline and revealed the cupulae and belltowers of the many churches of Assisi and finally the breathtaking Basilica of San Franscesco above its medieval arcading.

Philip had reserved rooms in the 'Hotel II Palazzo' in the Via San Franscesco, which was conveniently situated close to both the Basilica and the main square, the Piazza dei Comune. After checking in, they walked from the hotel into the Piazza dei Comune and found facing it the medieval buildings framing the Temple di Minerva, now converted into a church. They wandered in and out of the shops in the piazza, some of whose basements were opened to reveal Roman ruins. Like Perugia, the city of Assisi was compact and using the illustrated guide book they had bought in the tourist office, they strolled through roughly parallel streets, joined by flights of steps, discovering architectural gems that had little changed since medieval times, until they came across the Trattoria Dal Carro, off Corsa Mazzini and watched, as their food was prepared and then cooked over an open fire.

The next morning after they had checked out of the hotel, Philip drove his aunt and his sister to the car park in the Piazzale del 'Unita d'Italia' and from there they walked to the Basilica di San Franscecso and joined an English language tour led by an American Franciscan friar.

The priest took them first to the Sala delle Reliquie, where they saw items from St. Francis' life, including his simple tunic and sandals and fragments of the Canticle of the Creatures and the Franciscan Rule parchment, the 'Book of Life' composed by St. Francis. The friar was an enthusiastic guide, pointing out the stained glass windows of the lower church and the frescos over the main altar depicting St. Francis' victory over evil and the three precepts of his order based on obedience, poverty and chastity. He told them that the most accurate likeness of St. Francis was almost certainly the one of him in the painting of the 'Madonna in Majesty'. He took them to see the restoration work in progress on the frescos, which had been all but destroyed in the devastating earthquake in 1997; then he thanked them for coming to the Basilica and directed them to the bookshop, where they could buy postcards of the original paintings.

Outside the Basilica, they stood on the forecourt looking down on the city and across the valley to the imposing Rocco Maggiore.

"It's like stepping back into the Middle Ages," said Joan.

Just then an aircraft flew over, trailing a thin jet stream and the spell was broken.

Chapter 34

They arrived back at Philip's flat in the late evening. He checked his answer phone for messages. There was one from his office asking him to contact them in the morning and one from James Mulholland asking Susie to phone him on his mobile. They were all tired from the journey, but Philip's fridge was practically empty, so they settled on going to Enrico's again.

"We can have a light meal. Enrico won't mind. I sometimes just have antipasto and coffee," said Philip.

"Tomorrow's our last day," said Susie. "I would like to go into the city to buy presents to take back for Mum and Dad."

"OK. Let's eat; have an early night and I'll take you in with me in the morning."

"Thank you Philip. I'll go along with that," said Joan. "And Philip; thank you for taking me to Rimini."

"My pleasure, Aunt Joan."

"I'll drop you off by the Piazza de Fiori; you're bound to find something there. I'll meet you back at the flat as soon after one o'clock as I can manage. Buy something in the market for lunch and Susie; don't leave your packing until the last minute. Ciao."

"Philip is so sensible," said Susie. "I wish he would break out and do something mad once in a while."

"But then he wouldn't be Philip, would he?" said her aunt.

"I really don't know what to take back for Mum. She's already got so much stuff from here," Susie said, as they walked round the market. "Somewhere around here there is a shop called Baulla, where Mum used to buy presents for the girls in Dad's office."

"Yes, I remember your mother sending me some really beautiful gloves from there one Christmas."

"Time's getting on. We'll go there first and then buy something for lunch in the Campo di Fiori and then make a dash back to the flat."

"Are you sure you have everything? Passports – tickets?"

"Yes Philip. I've checked."

"Aunt Joan?"

"Yes Philip."

"Come ON Philip. I want time to look round the duty free shop. If we wait much longer we won't catch the plane."

They arrived at the airport with time to spare and checked in their luggage. Susie was all set to say 'goodbye' to Philip and go through Passport Control, but he seemed to be hanging back for some reason, until he saw the tall figure of James hurrying through the concourse towards them and raised his hand.

"There's James," he said unnecessarily.

"What's he doing here?"

"Ask him. Aunt Joan, shall we see if we can get some coffee?"

"Well James, what are you doing here?"

"I left a message on Philip's answer phone and when you didn't ring me I phoned him at his office and asked him what time your plane was leaving."

"And?"

"I wanted to see you again before you went home. I had hoped to take you out to dinner on your own."

"Why? To see if the ugly duckling really had turned into a swan?"

"Susan, please listen. I wanted to tell you that I'm being posted back to London. That evening when we met by the Spanish Steps, I fell in love with you all over again."

"You never were in love with me."

"Yes I was, but you were going away to university and I had just begun my career in the Diplomatic Corps. It wasn't the right time."

"And now it is?"

"I hope so Susan. At least let's keep in touch until I take up my new appointment. When I'm based in London, we can really get to know each other again."

"That's my flight being called. There's Philip and Aunt Joan. I must go."

"I'll call you when you get home. I have your father's number."

They walked towards Passport Control together and before Susie went through, James took her by the shoulders and bent his head and kissed her. "Please Susan. Darling?"

Smiling up at him, she said, "See you in London then James."

She blew him a kiss and watched as a delighted grin spread across his face like a flower opening in slow motion.

'Three cheers for the Trevi Fountain,' thought Susie.

"That was nice of James to come and see you off at the airport, wasn't it?" said Joan when they had settled themselves on the plane.

"Yes, wasn't it?"

"I knew a James once. He was a sergeant in the Green Howards Regiment. He was the brother of a teaching colleague, Molly Erskine. He was home on leave and his family were celebrating his birthday and Molly asked me along to the party. James and I hit it off straight away and we fell in love. When he went back to his regiment, we wrote to each other and sometimes, at weekends, I used to go and stay at a hotel near the barracks. Then his unit was sent back to Ireland to do a final tour of duty. I wanted us to get married before he left, but James was planning on leaving the army and wanted us to wait until he came back and his future was more settled. But he never did come back. He was killed in an IRA ambush."

"I'm sorry Aunt Joan. I didn't know."

"It was before you were born. I had other relationships, but none like James and then my mother died suddenly and I stayed at home to look after my father until he died. Are you in love with James?"

"I don't know."

"He seems very fond of you. I like him. Will you keep in touch with him?"

"Yes, I think so. He's really rather a sweetie under all that starchy formality."

Chapter 35

Robert was waiting for them when Joan and Susie arrived at Gatwick Airport in the late evening. They had gone straight to bed when they reached Robert's home in Highgate Village, but now after a good night's rest, Joan was ready to talk to him and his wife, Jenny, about what had happened when she had met Paolo in Rimini.

Long after they had finished breakfast, they remained seated at the table talking. Joan told them how they had come upon a bar run by Vincente Cardi, one of Paolo's sons, and that Vincente's daughter, Carmela, had been serving in the bar and had spoken to them in English, the first evening they had arrived in Rimini and then on the second evening, she had taken them along to meet Paolo.

"What did he say when you met him?" asked Robert.

"He didn't give much away actually," said Susie. "Philip told him that it was Jessie and Jack Cummings who wished to be remembered to him and he seemed to accept that."

"But when I went to see him on my own the next evening," Joan continued, "he told me that he knew there was more to the story and asked after Lizzie. When I told him that she had died he asked me if I knew why Lizzie had not replied to his letters and I had to tell him that she had never received them. And then he said that although he had married, he had never forgotten Lizzie and that his daughter was actually called Elisabetta."

"I've been thinking a lot about those letters while you were in Italy," Jenny said. "I don't think it was your mother who kept them from Lizzie. I think it was Granny Piper."

"What makes you think that?" Robert asked.

"Think about it. Times were very different then. An illegitimate baby, particularly one whose father was a foreigner and an Italian prisoner of war at that, wouldn't have been something to broadcast, would it? There was a lot more prejudice against unmarried mothers then. Granny Piper was a bit of a Puritan, by all accounts, and although she was prepared for Lizzie to stay on at the farm, I don't think she would have taken kindly to the idea of Paolo being the father."

"Yes, what was it that Jessie said – 'Mrs. Piper was a bit tight-lipped about it'?" said Susie.

"Remember your mother only kept the letters locked away. The birth certificate and the photo weren't with them. I don't think she found them when she brought the bureau from the farm."

"But she must have known about the birth certificate," Joan said.

"She probably thought that Lizzie had it. You said that it was stuck in a groove at the back of the bureau drawer; she might only have found the letters. Did you ask Signor Cardi when he wrote the first letter, Joan?"

"No I didn't."

"So we don't really know when the letters started arriving. Perhaps they didn't come until long after Lizzie had left the farm to begin her teacher training."

"But why did she leave her baby with our mother?" asked Robert.

"It must have seemed the ideal solution at the time. She knew the baby would be well looked after. Your mother was very soft-hearted and I think when she saw how desolate Lizzie was, she wanted to help her get on with her life."

"Why didn't she take me to be with her later on?"

"Probably because by that time you were settled and happy with your surrogate family and Lizzie decided for your sake to leave things as they were."

"I don't suppose we shall ever know for certain what happened, but I must say that seems a more likely story," said Robert. "I really don't think our mother would have kept the letters from Lizzie when they first started coming, if she had known about them. She had left the farm herself when Dad was de-mobbed and he had started working at 'The Chronicle' and they had set up home in London, bringing Lizzie's baby with them. Granny Piper must have thought she was doing the right thing for all concerned in the circumstances."

"Did Signor Cardi realise that you were his and Lizzie's child?" asked Jenny

"I told him I was Lizzie's daughter when I gave him the St. Christopher medallion that he had given to Lizzie as a love token, before he was repatriated. He said I was like Lizzie, but that I was also like his daughter, Elisabetta, and then he gave the medallion back to me and asked me to keep it for the love of him as well as Lizzie. He held me in his arms for a moment and then we kissed 'goodbye'."

"Did you meet his wife – other members of his family?" Robert asked.

"No. We only met Vincente and Carmela. Elisabetta had had a new baby boy and his wife was away visiting her. He didn't even tell me her name. There was another son, Paolo, but we didn't see him either."

"Shall you keep in touch?"

"No. I don't think so Robert. He was very kind, but rather reserved, understandably so, being confronted with a fifty-four year old daughter he knew nothing about. He was my natural father, it's true, but Mum and Dad were my loving parents and..." she came round the table and put her arms around him and kissed him, "you'll always be my big brother."

His answering kiss was one of relief.

"Did you enjoy your time in Italy?" asked Jenny. "Rome is such a stimulating city. I loved every minute of our time at the Embassy."

"Yes, I did. It was lovely being with the children again. Almost like old times, except that this time I felt they were in charge of me. And before we came home we went to Baulla and bought presents for you both."

"And to Castroni's," said Susie, bringing the gift-wrapped basket of delicacies to the table.

"How lovely," said her mother. "I think receiving presents is one of the nicest parts of family returning from holiday."

Robert smiled at his wife as she opened the gifts and turning to Joan, he said, "Happier now Joanie? Everything settled?"

"Yes Robert. That was some legacy Cousin Lizzie left me, but everything's settled now."

Some weeks after his aunt and his sister had returned home, Philip stopped at the reception desk of his office to collect his mail. The receptionist was new and Philip smiled and said, "Buon giorno."

The girl returned his smile and replied, "Buon Giorno Signor Lewis."

'There's something familiar about this girl,' he thought.

He glanced at her name badge and read 'Carmela Cardi'.

"I believe we have met before," he said.

Epilogue: Lizzie's Story

You can never go back. Isn't that what they say? Lizzie sat in an armchair in a room which overlooked the hospice gardens, thinking back over her life, which she knew was drawing to its close. Would she have changed anything?

She had put her affairs in order. Joan would be surprised to learn that her father's 'Cousin' Lizzie had left her a tidy sum of money; enough to buy herself a place of her own. After all she felt she owed the girl something. Few people outside of Elmersdale knew that Joan was the love-child resulting from her wartime liaison with an Italian prisoner of war and those who had known, had kept her secret.

Memories of the day she and Jessie Silverton had met at the Women's Land Army Training Centre came flooding back. They had both just turned eighteen years old and coming from similar backgrounds, had become friends. She shivered involuntarily, remembering the bitterly cold day in early January 1942 when they had been met at Elmersdale Station and taken to 'Piper's Farm' by the farmer's daughter, Anne Lewis. What a fortunate coincidence that had turned out to be – since they shared the same surname. Anne was married to a serving army officer and while her husband was away, fighting in the Middle East, she and her baby boy had remained at her parents' farm.

She remembered how after the four weeks' training, the two of them had thought they could cope with anything they would have to do on the farm. How wrong they had been. The hours had been long and the work back-breaking at times, but she and Jessie were determined not to let Mr. Piper and his farmhand, Ben, know how ill-prepared they were. They had stuck at it, uncomplaining, except to each other, as they ministered to their blistered hands and aching limbs. Mrs. Piper had looked after them well and although she could be brusque at times, they had felt she had their best interests at heart.

A smile crossed Lizzie's face. What was that daft song she and Jessie used to sing? She began to sing softly to herself.

She volunteered to be a Land Girl,
She thought the life would be a whirl.
Ten bob a week.

"That wasn't right. It was twenty-eight shillings."

Nothing much to eat.

"That wasn't right either. Mrs. Piper had fed them well."

Great big boots that gave her blisters on her feet.
She volunteered to be a Land Girl,
She thought the life would be a whirl.
If it wasn't for the war, she'd be where she was before.

"Stuck in some dusty old solicitor's office."

And then if they were out of earshot, they would shout the last line. *Land Girl, you're barmy* before dissolving into helpless laughter.

She supposed they had been a bit barmy, but they had been young and in spite of everything that had happened later, the years at the farm had been happy ones and she and Jessie had been such good friends.

"I wonder where she is now?" she thought. "I should have made more effort to keep in touch."

And then there was Paolo. He was one of six Italian POWs that Mr. Piper had been allocated to help out at harvest time. In her mind's eye she saw again the tall, darkly handsome, young man and remembered his attempts to engage her in conversation, in his limited English, when she and Jessie had brought down the baskets of food from the farmhouse for the prisoners to eat, as they took a break from working. The sergeant, who was there to supervise the POWs, had taken a fancy to Jessie and so, sometimes, she and Paolo were left alone together.

She recalled the day Paolo had shown her a picture of the little town of Rimini, where he came from, and had pointed out the cafe on the sea front that belonged to his father. She remembered that she had given Paolo pencils and a writing pad and had helped him with his English and he had drawn her pictures of the beach and the fishing boats.

She relived the day that Mr. Piper had given a farewell party for the POWs who had worked for him, shortly before they were to be repatriated, after Italy had made peace with the Allies. It had been quite a gathering. As well as the Italians and their guards, Ben and his brother Tom, the Pipers' pre-war farmhand, on leave from the army, had been there and friends and members of the Pipers' family too. She and Paolo had managed to slip away unnoticed. They had gone to the hayloft in the barn and there they had made love for the first and last time. Paolo had told her that he loved her and wanted to marry her. He had kissed her tenderly and given her his St. Christopher medallion as a token of his love.

"Oh, Paolo, I was so happy then. Why didn't you write to me as you had promised? I would have waited for you, no matter how long it took."

She felt again the panic when she realised that she was pregnant not long after Paolo had returned home. She knew that Ben was in love with her. He would have married her to save her from being disgraced and brought up the baby as his own, but she hadn't wanted that. Ben was too young to be saddled with a wife and baby and then, she had still hoped that Paolo would send for her. And so she had waited for the longed-for letter. And waited. And waited. Her baby girl, named Joan after her dead mother, had been born at the end of May 1945 and still there was no word from Paolo.

After the birth of her baby, Lizzie had stayed on at 'Piper's Farm' for a while, but when the war finally ended, Lizzie knew she wouldn't be able to stay for much longer. Jessie had married her sergeant; Tom had been demobbed and had come back to work for Mr. Piper and Anne was still living at the farm, while she waited for her husband to return home.

"What shall I do?" she had thought. "Where can I go?"

The day Anne had shown her the government notice in a daily paper asking for service personnel to apply for a one-year teacher training course, had been the spur she needed. She remembered the excitement she had felt when her application had been accepted and had been grateful when Anne had kindly offered to look after Joan until she had completed the course. She had thought that gaining her teaching certificate would mean the beginning of a new life for her and her baby. Finding somewhere to live had proved something of a problem and she was lucky to find a bed-sitting room, but the landlady had stipulated no animals and no children.

By this time, Anne's husband had been de-mobbed and was now a journalist working on his father's newspaper. He and Anne were living with his parents in their spacious house in Canonbury, so once again Lizzie had accepted Anne's offer to look after her baby. As time went by and Joan became more settled with her surrogate family, Lizzie had made the difficult decision to leave her in the care of Anne and Edward Lewis and to be brought up with their little boy, Robert. Although she could never quite bring herself to let them adopt Joan, Lizzie could see the advantage of her having a family life, rather than being put into a day nursery while she was teaching. That was when she had given the birth certificate and the photo of her and Paolo into Anne's keeping; to be given to her daughter some time in the future, if ever the occasion arose.

"I thought it was the right thing to do at the time," she said aloud.

Her thoughts turned again to Paolo. When restrictions on foreign travel had eased up after the war, she had gone on holiday to Rimini with some colleagues. She had found the Trattoria Marina on the sea front and had observed Paolo working, but had not made herself known to him. She had seen the woman she supposed was his wife, hugely pregnant and with two small boys in tow. She remembered how angry she had felt with herself for being so naive and angry and hurt that Paolo had not kept his promise to her. She had vowed then that no man would make a fool of her ever again.

She returned from that holiday determined to concentrate on her teaching career and in time had become the respected headmistress of a prestigious London girls' school.

She had kept in touch with Anne Lewis over the years and was sad when she had received the letter telling her that she had died and inviting her to the memorial service, to be held in St. Philip's in Elmersdale. At the service she had been introduced as Cousin Lizzie and when she had come face to face with the daughter she had given up, so many years ago, she knew that she had made the right decision. She hoped that if Joan ever became aware of the relationship, she would understand.

She closed her eyes and saw again Paolo's smiling, handsome face. With hindsight, would she have changed anything?

Perhaps. Who knows? That was life.

BIBLIOGRAPHY

Hutchinson's *Factfinder Concise Encyclopaedia*

The Land Girls by Angela Huth

Reader's Digest – *Yesterday's Britain*

Cresta – Travel Brochure

Citalia – Travel Brochure

Collins Italian Phrase Book and Dictionary

Collins – Italian CD

Lonely Planet – *Best of Rome*

Lonely Planet – *Tuscany and Umbria*

Eye-witness Travel Guides: *Rimini* pages 258 & 557